ADVENTURE TIME™

BANANA GUARD ACADEMY

ADVENTURE TIME™ created by PENDLETON WARD

ADVENTURE TIME: BANANA GUARD ACADEMY, June 2015. Published by KaBOOM!, a division of Boom Entertainment, Inc.

A catalog record of this book is available from OCLC and from the KaBOOM! website, www.kaboom-studios.com, on the Librarians Page.

BOOM! Studios, 5670 Wilshire Boulevard, Suite 450, Los Angeles, CA 90036-5679. Printed in China. First Printing.

ISBN: 978-1-60886-486-7, eISBN: 978-1-61398-340-9

Written by

KENT OSBORNE & DYLAN HAGGERTY

Illustrated by

MAD RUPERT

Colors by
WHITNEY COGAR

Letters by
LEIGH LUNA

"I LOVE TO PARTY"
Illustrated by
BRITT WILSON

Cover by
PERRY MAPLE

Designer
JILLIAN CRAB

Associate Editor
WHITNEY LEOPARD

Editor
SHANNON WATTERS

With Special Thanks to Marisa Marionakis, Rick Blanco, Nicole Rivera, Conrad Montgomery, Meghan Bradley, Curtis Lelash, Kelly Crews and the wonderful folks at Cartoon Network.

CHAPTER ONE

INSOMNIA IS OFTEN CAUSED BY INSUFFICIENT LEVELS OF MELATONIN IN THE BRAIN.
EATING FOODS RICH IN TRYPTOPHAN CAN GENERATE SEROTONIN, WHICH ENZYMES IN THE BRAIN CATALYZE INTO MELATONIN.
A TURNIP SANDWICH OUGHTA DO THE TRICK.
HOW ?

TURNIPS... TURNIPS... TURNIPS...

HUH. GUESS I'M OUT OF TURNIPS.
SHUT

LUCKILY I KNOW WHERE THERE'S TONS OF FOOD.
JINGL JANGL
CLICK
THE BIG FRID
THE BANANA GUARD COMMISSARY!
FWOOOOSH
HMM...NO TURNIPS IN HERE EITHER? THAT CAN'T BE RIGHT.
CAN I HELP YOU WITH SOMETHING PRINCESS?
SHUT
OH, CAPTAIN ROOT BEER GU I DIDN'T SEE YOU THER
I WAS BEHIN THE DOOR.
I CAN'T SEEM TO FIND ANY TURNIPS.
OH WE NEVER HAVE SPARE TURNIPS, PRINCESS.
WHAT? WHY?
YOU KNOW... ON ACCOUNT OF THE BANANA GUARDS.

BANANA GUARDS LOVE TURNIPS. IT'S ALL THEY EAT.
ALL THEY EAT?!
WHAT ABOUT POTATOES? DON'T THEY EAT POTATOES?
NOPE.
TAPE
BROCCOLI?
NOPE.
EGGS?
NOPE.
PEAS?
NO, PRINCESS.
CHEESE?
NO, THEY DON'T LIKE CHEESE.
CAPTAIN ROOT BEER GUY, I THINK THE BANANA GUARD NEEDS TO DIVERSIFY. OTHERWISE WE'RE NEVER GONNA GET RID OF ALL THIS FOOD.
Hmm...
PRINCESS, YOU LOOK LIKE YOU'RE GONNA MAKE A BIG--

"--ANNOUNCEMENT."
CITIZENS OF THE CANDY KINGDOM
EFFECTIVE IMMEDIATELY, I HAVE ORDERED
COMMANDANT BANANA GUARD
TO OPEN THE GATES OF THE
BANANA GUARD ACADEMY
TO ALL NON-BANANA CITIZENS
THAT WISH TO SERVE!
CITIZENS WHO LOVE TURNIPS
NEED NOT APPLY.
THANK YOU!
I LOVE YOU!

great speech, Princess!
THANKS, PEP BUT.
UH... PRINCESS?
YES, ROOT BEER GUY?
I'M WONDERING HOW THIS WILL AFFECT THE FORCE?
ELL FOR STARTERS, JE'RE GOING TO TTRACT RECRUITS...
PAP!
...WHO LIKE TO EAT THINGS OTHER THAN TURNIPS.
WILL IT STILL BE CALLED THE BANANA GUARD?
Princess?
UH... YEAH. I MEAN. I GUESS SO.
i like things other than turnips.
HAHA, YES I KNOW, LIKE TACOS. YOU LOVE TACOS.
yes, but what i'm trying to tell you is that i'd like to enroll.
THAT'S GREAT, PEP BUT!
you don't mind?
OF COURSE NOT!
WOW, THAT'S REALLY SOMETHING. I WONDER WHO ELSE WANTS TO JOIN...

!
NEWS TIME!!!
BREAKING NEWS!!! IN THE CANDY KINGDOM!
HEY
PAGE 10
NON-BANANAS ALLOWED IN THE BG THIS COULDN'T POSSIBLY GO
It finally happened!
YOU TOO COULD BE A
WHAT FINALLY HAPPENED, DEAR?
I'm finally going to realize my lifelong dream of becoming a Banana Guard.
I THOUGHT YOUR DREAM WAS A BIGGER HOUSE.
I have lots of dreams.
Would you help me with this please?
HA HA, WELL SINCE YOU ASKED NICELY.
I always ask nicely.
YOU GOT ME THERE, SWEET T.

OH MY! IT'S...IT'S...
AN OLD TIN CAN?
I made this when I was a little girl.
How do I look?
WELL, LIKE A MILLION BUCKS! But...BUT...
I GUESS I'M GONNA BE A BANANA GUARD'S WIFE?
hmm, I didn't make anything else.
I MEAN, ON THE ONE HAND, I'M SUPER PROUD YOU'LL BE PROTECTING THE KINGDOM...
...BUT ON THE OTHER HAND I KNOW I'M GONNA BE SUPER WORRIED WHEN YOU'RE OUT FIGHTING CRIMES.
I'm surprised I didn't make some handcuffs out of rubber bands. That would've been easy.
Not even a baton?

I JUST NEED YOU TO ANSWER ONE QUESTION!
What?
WHY IS ROOT BEER GUY LOOKING IN OUR WINDOW?!
DON'T MIND ME, FOLKS!
BOY, TREE TRUNKS! WHO'DA THUNK IT? OKAY, SO HER AND PEPPERMINT BUTLER...
... I WONDER IF ANYONE ELSE IS THINKING ABOUT--
I'M GONNA JOIN THE BANANA GUARD!!!

MR. CUPCAKE?! YOU TOO?
DON'T TELL ME YOU MADE A SAD HAT OUT OF A TIN CAN WHEN YOU WERE A KID...
TIN CAN HAT? NO. NO MY REASONS ARE DIFFERENT. MY REASONS...
... ARE FOR LOVE
0 YEARS AGO.
UN EDROIT AGRÉABLE
AGRÉABLE
FLASH!
Trés bien. I will have zee picture for you by zee end of zee meal.
THIS PLACE IS SO AGREEABLE.

Hee Hee! The flash blinded me!
Ho Ho! ME AS WELL!
BUT NO FLASH CAN OUTSHINE... ...YOUR BEAUTY.
Mr. Cupcake, stop. I told you we're just friends.
BUT... I WANT TO BE MORE THAN FRIENDS.
You know my father will only allow me to date Banana Guards. Now let's order.
FINE.
SO IF I JOINED THE BANANA GUARD YOU'D GO OUT WITH ME?
You can't join the Banana Guard. You're a cupcake.
NO NO, ANSWER THE QUESTION.
Well... yes. But...
AHH! BUTS ARE FOR POOPING!
haha...
Well this is me.
I'M GOING TO BECOME A BANANA GUARD! YOU MARK MY WORDS!
heh heh. whatever.
YOU MARK MY WORDS!

THE NEXT DAY
RIIIIIPP!!!
HEY YOU! NEED A LAWYER??
Your highness, what makes someone a Banana?
CANDY COUR
I DO. I MADE ALL THE BANANAS AND I MADE YOU.
Yes but--
JUDGE B.GUM
BUTS ARE FOR POOPING.
CLAK!
DENIED.
I WILL CONTINUE TO FIGHT!
BANANA GUARDS
UN-FAIR

PSSSHH
FAIR
ARGH!
YOU'VE MISSED THREE DAYS OF WORK! YOU'RE FIRED!
Cupcake! Pick up the phone, buddy! Forget about that dumb banana. Come bowling with us tonight. It'll be fun!
THE LANES
SHOES
THE LANES
THE LANES
BACK TO TODAY
AND THEY WERE RIGHT. IT WAS FUN. AND I FORGOT ALL ABOUT THAT DUMB BANANA.
UNTIL TODAY.
GEE, I WONDER WHO ELSE IS THINKING OF JOINING.

SETTLE DOWN, CHILDREN.
OH DEAR.
BOP
CALL
THEY'RE NOT USING THEIR LISTENING HATS!
MR. GINGERBREAD MUTO, WILL YOU PLEASE COME IN HERE AND HELP ME?
INTERCOM
CALL
POMPF
QUIET!

It's time to Play
Red Light, Green Light.

YAYYY!

Red Light!
FREEZE!

20 MINUTES LATER

aren't you gonna say
"green light?"

You Broke the Rules.
YOU'RE OUT.
aw.

Red Light!

OH YOU'RE SO GOOD WITH THE CHILDREN!
WOULD YOU EVER CONSIDER JOINING US FULL TIME?
HMM.
Well to be honest, I've always had a different dream job...
... a job where I could make a difference.
HOP
HOP
HOP
AM I... SHOULD I JUST FOLLOW YOU?
...Where I could really express myself.
BROKEN!!
STOP.
BUS
MAIL
RED LIGHT!

But we both know they'd never accept a ginger like me.
MR. GINGERBREAD MUTO, YOU NEED TO CATCH UP ON CURRENT EVENTS.
BANAGUARD ACA LETTING NON-BANANA'S IN WHAT'S UP WI THAT??
JOIN NOW
SPORTS
I GUESS
RBG: "SHRUG"
HM?
LOOKS LIKE YOU CAN ACHIEVE YOUR DREAM AFTER ALL!
MR. GINGERBREAD MUTO?
AH HA HA HA!!! I'M GOING TO BANANA GUARD ACADEMY!
Green Light!
YOYYYYYYYYYYYYYY!!!!
OH DEAR.
YOUNG MAN ARE YOU GOOD WITH CHILDREN?
HAHA! DON'T MIND ME. I'M JUST NARRATING!
OKAY, SO...THAT GUY, MR.CUPCAKE, TREE TRUNKS AND PEPPERMINT BUTLER. BOY, THAT'S REALLY SOMETHING. I WONDER IF THERE WILL BE OTHERS?

Lollipop Girl

PINEAPPLE
GUY

TAFFY GIRL!

UNCLE
CHEWY

Gumdrop Lass

CANDY
HEART
TUG
ME

CHET

MARSHMALLOW
KID

BANANA GUARD ACADEMY
GOSH, THE NEXT TIME THESE GATES ARE OPEN, THERE'S GONNA BE ALL SORTS OF FOLKS PASSING THROUGH.
KRA-KOOOM
BANANA GUARD ACADEMY
SO MANY PEOPLE PURSUING THEIR DREAMS.
KINDA MAKES YOU FEEL HAPPY INSIDE.

PUNCHY in
I LOVE TO PARTY
WRITTEN BY: KENT OSBORNE + DYLAN HAGGERTY
ILLUSTRATED BY: BRITT WILSON
PARTY!
PARTY!
PARTY!
KISS
PARTY!

PARTY!

PARTYYY!

PARTY!

HAPPY BIRTHDAY!
PARTY!

PARTY!

CRASH!
!
MY LIFE'S WORK!
WHOMP.
SORRY BRAH.
PARTY?

I'LL TAKE IT FROM HERE.

LOOK PUNCHY, YOU'RE MY FAVORITE, SO I'M GONNA MAKE YOU A DEAL.

YOU CAN EITHER GO TO JAIL, OR ENROLL IN THE BANANA GUARD ACADEMY
AND TRY TO MAKE SOMETHING OF YOUR LIFE.
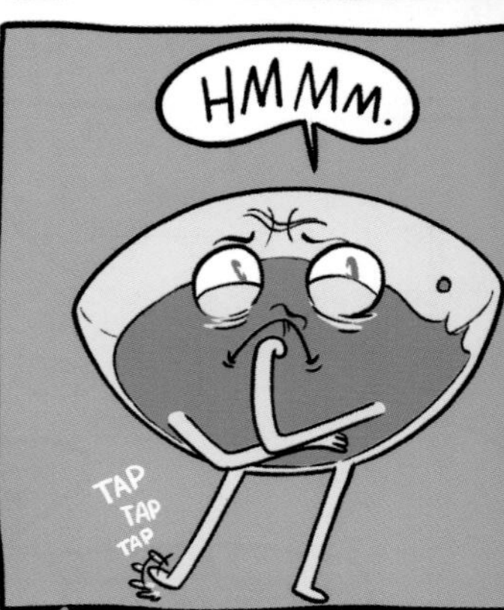
HMMM.
TAP TAP TAP

SLAM

PARTY!
THE END.

CHAPTER TWO

CHOMP!
DO YOU KNOW
HAT TODAY IS?
NO, OF COURSE YOU DON'T.
IT'S THE FIRST DAY OF SCHOOL FOR THE 218th CLASS OF HER ROYAL MAJESTY'S BANANA GUARD ACADEMY.

I REMEMBER MY FIRST DAY AT THE ACADEMY.
IT WAS RAINING, AND I WAS LATE LEAVING MY HOUSE, SO I RAN AS FAST AS I COULD DOWN COBBLER LANE.
...I TRIPPED OVER A ROOT AND FELL DOWN, INSTINCTIVELY PROTECTING MY SCHOOL BOOKS INSTEAD OF MY FACE.
TUNK!
OH SURE, I MAY HAVE BLOODIED MY NOSE AND SHATTERED THREE TEETH THAT MORNING.
BUT YOU KNOW WHAT?
MMMISS!
I MADE IT TO THE ACADEMY
POK
POK
ON TIME.
I WAS TWO YEARS OLD.

SINCE THEN I'VE DEDICATED MY LIFE TO THE GUARD.
QUICKLY RISING THROUGH THE RANKS LIKE A FEARLESS MOUNTAIN GOAT.
I WAS THE YOUNGEST BANANA TO EVER MAKE CAPTAIN.
TO THIS DAY I HAVE NO IDEA WHAT I DID WRONG.
GLAK
. . .
HAVE YOU NOTHING TO SAY ?!?

HUH? WERE YOU TALKING TO ME THIS WHOLE TIME?
YES! OF COURSE! WHO'D YOU THINK I WAS TALKING TO? MY FISH?
I THOUGHT MAYBE YOU WERE NARRATING.
"NARRATING"? WHAT DO YOU MEAN?
YOU KNOW, LIKE I WAS DOING IN THE LAST ISSUE.
I CAN TAKE IT FROM HERE, CAPTAIN ROOT BEER GUY.
YES, OF COURSE. I'LL LEAVE YOU TO IT.
SO SORRY AGAIN ABOUT TAKING YOUR JOB.
HMMF
AND I'M SO SORRY THAT I'LL BE FAILING ALL OF PRINCESS BUBBLEGUM'S NEW RECRUITS.

WHAT WAS THAT?
Mm?
GET OUT OF HERE!
ZIP!
GRUMBLE GRUMBLE
and then, after you go to the quartermaster... "all new recruits are instructed to... report to the classroom for... orien...tation."
I DID IT!
Oh I can't believe it's actually happening.
can i see the basement?
ARE WE OFFICIALLY BANANA GUARDS NOW?
When do we get our spears?
Z Z

JEEZ, ONLY ONE GUY WORKING THE BOOTH? THIS IS GOING TO TAKE FOREVER.
I'VE WAITED THIS LONG.
your glasses are pretty.
Thanks, Tree Trunks.
We're not getting spears?
here are some clothes for exercising.
UNIFORMS
TUG ME
Where is the basement?
Okay everyone, Please take a seat.
There's a piece of paper on your desk, but don't flip it over yet.

Okay, you may now
lip your papers over.
Don't worry, it's not a test. It's just a *questionnaire*.
LIP. flip. flip. FLIP. flip.
You have 30 minutes to complete the test -- I mean *questionnaire*... starting...
...now!
SMART BANANAS MAKE GOOD GUARDS
THERE!

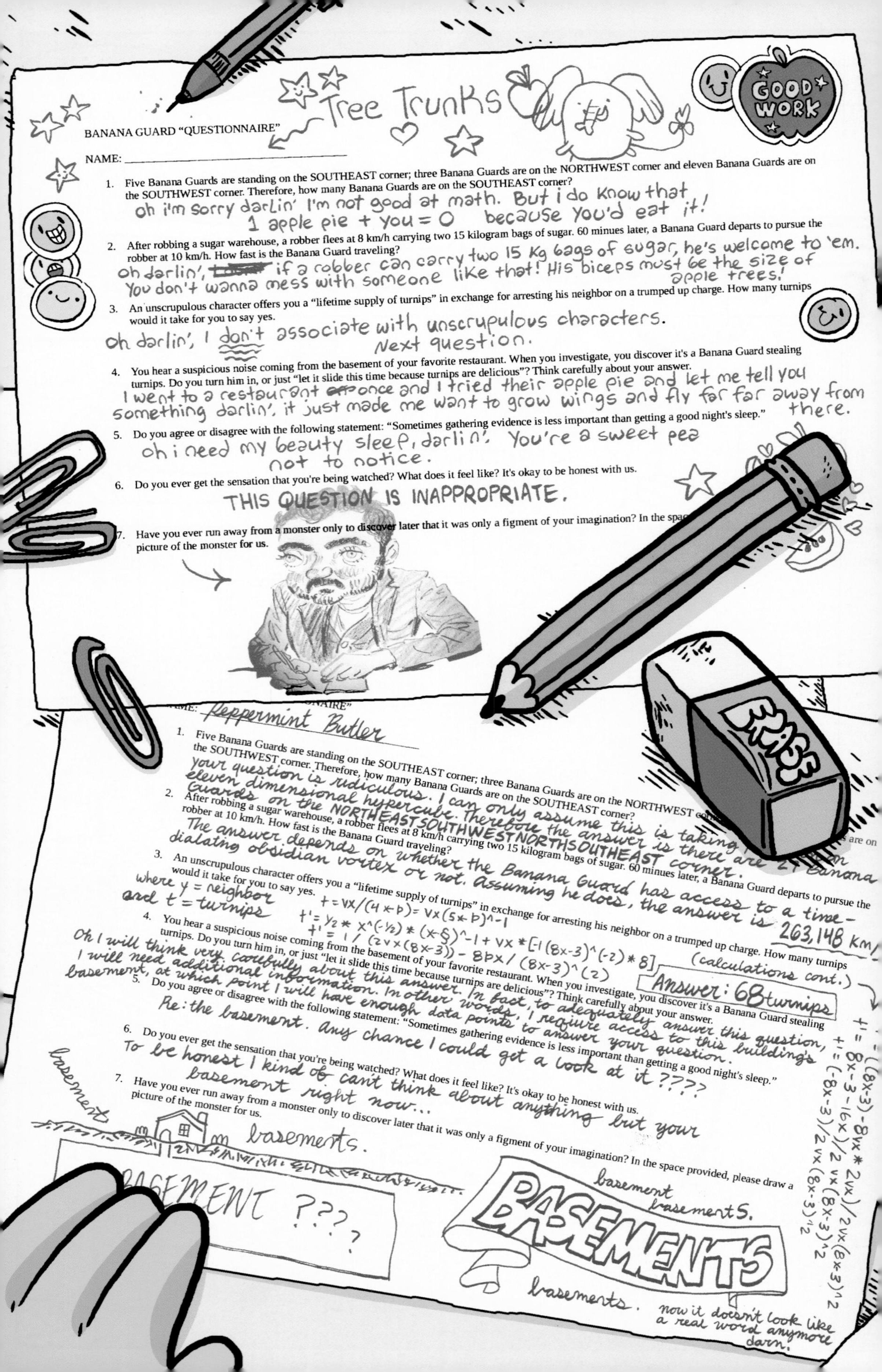
BANANA GUARD "QUESTIONNAIRE"
Tree Trunks
GOOD WORK
NAME:
1. Five Banana Guards are standing on the SOUTHEAST corner; three Banana Guards are on the NORTHWEST corner and eleven Banana Guards are on the SOUTHWEST corner. Therefore, how many Banana Guards are on the SOUTHEAST corner?
oh i'm sorry darlin' I'm not good at math. But i do know that 1 apple pie + you = 0 because you'd eat it!
2. After robbing a sugar warehouse, a robber flees at 8 km/h carrying two 15 kilogram bags of sugar. 60 minues later, a Banana Guard departs to pursue the robber at 10 km/h. How fast is the Banana Guard traveling?
oh darlin', if a robber can carry two 15 Kg bags of sugar, he's welcome to 'em. You don't wanna mess with someone like that! His biceps must be the size of apple trees!
3. An unscrupulous character offers you a "lifetime supply of turnips" in exchange for arresting his neighbor on a trumped up charge. How many turnips would it take for you to say yes.
oh darlin', I don't associate with unscrupulous characters. Next question.
4. You hear a suspicious noise coming from the basement of your favorite restaurant. When you investigate, you discover it's a Banana Guard stealing turnips. Do you turn him in, or just "let it slide this time because turnips are delicious"? Think carefully about your answer.
I went to a restaurant once and I tried their apple pie and let me tell you something darlin', it just made me want to grow wings and fly far far away from there.
5. Do you agree or disagree with the following statement: "Sometimes gathering evidence is less important than getting a good night's sleep."
oh i need my beauty sleep, darlin'. You're a sweet pea not to notice.
6. Do you ever get the sensation that you're being watched? What does it feel like? It's okay to be honest with us.
THIS QUESTION IS INAPPROPRIATE.
7. Have you ever run away from a monster only to discover later that it was only a figment of your imagination? In the spa
picture of the monster for us.
NAME: Peppermint Butler
1. Five Banana Guards are standing on the SOUTHEAST corner; three Banana Guards are on the NORTHWEST corner and eleven Banana Guards are on the SOUTHWEST corner. Therefore, how many Banana Guards are on the SOUTHEAST corner?
your question is ridiculous. I can only assume this is taking place in an eleven dimensional hypercube. Therefore the answer is there are 27 Banana Guards on the NORTHEASTSOUTHWESTNORTHSOUTHEAST corner.
2. After robbing a sugar warehouse, a robber flees at 8 km/h carrying two 15 kilogram bags of sugar. 60 minues later, a Banana Guard departs to pursue the robber at 10 km/h. How fast is the Banana Guard traveling?
The answer depends on whether the Banana Guard has access to a time-dialating obsidian vortex or not. Assuming he does, the answer is 263,148 km/h
3. An unscrupulous character offers you a "lifetime supply of turnips" in exchange for arresting his neighbor on a trumped up charge. How many turnips would it take for you to say yes.
where y = neighbor and t = turnips
t = vx/(4*b) = vx(5*b)^-1
t' = 1/2 * x^(-1/2) * (x-§)^-1 + vx * [-1(8x-3)^(-2) * 8]
t' = 1/(2vx(8x-3)) - 8bx/(8x-3)^(2)
(calculations cont.)
t' = ((8x-3)-8vx * 2vx)/2vx(8x-3)^2
t' = 8x-3-16x)/2vx(8x-3)^2
t' = (-8x-3)/2vx(8x-3)^2
Answer: 68 turnips
4. You hear a suspicious noise coming from the basement of your favorite restaurant. When you investigate, you discover it's a Banana Guard stealing turnips. Do you turn him in, or just "let it slide this time because turnips are delicious"? Think carefully about your answer.
Oh I will think very carefully about this answer. In fact, to adequately answer this question, I will need additional information. In other words, I require access to this building's basement, at which point I will have enough data points to answer your question.
5. Do you agree or disagree with the following statement: "Sometimes gathering evidence is less important than getting a good night's sleep."
Re: the basement. Any chance I could get a look at it????
6. Do you ever get the sensation that you're being watched? What does it feel like? It's okay to be honest with us.
To be honest I kind of can't think about anything but your basement right now...
7. Have you ever run away from a monster only to discover later that it was only a figment of your imagination? In the space provided, please draw a picture of the monster for us.
basements
basements.
BASEMENT ???
basement
basements.
BASEMENTS
basements.
now it doesn't look like a real word anymore darn.

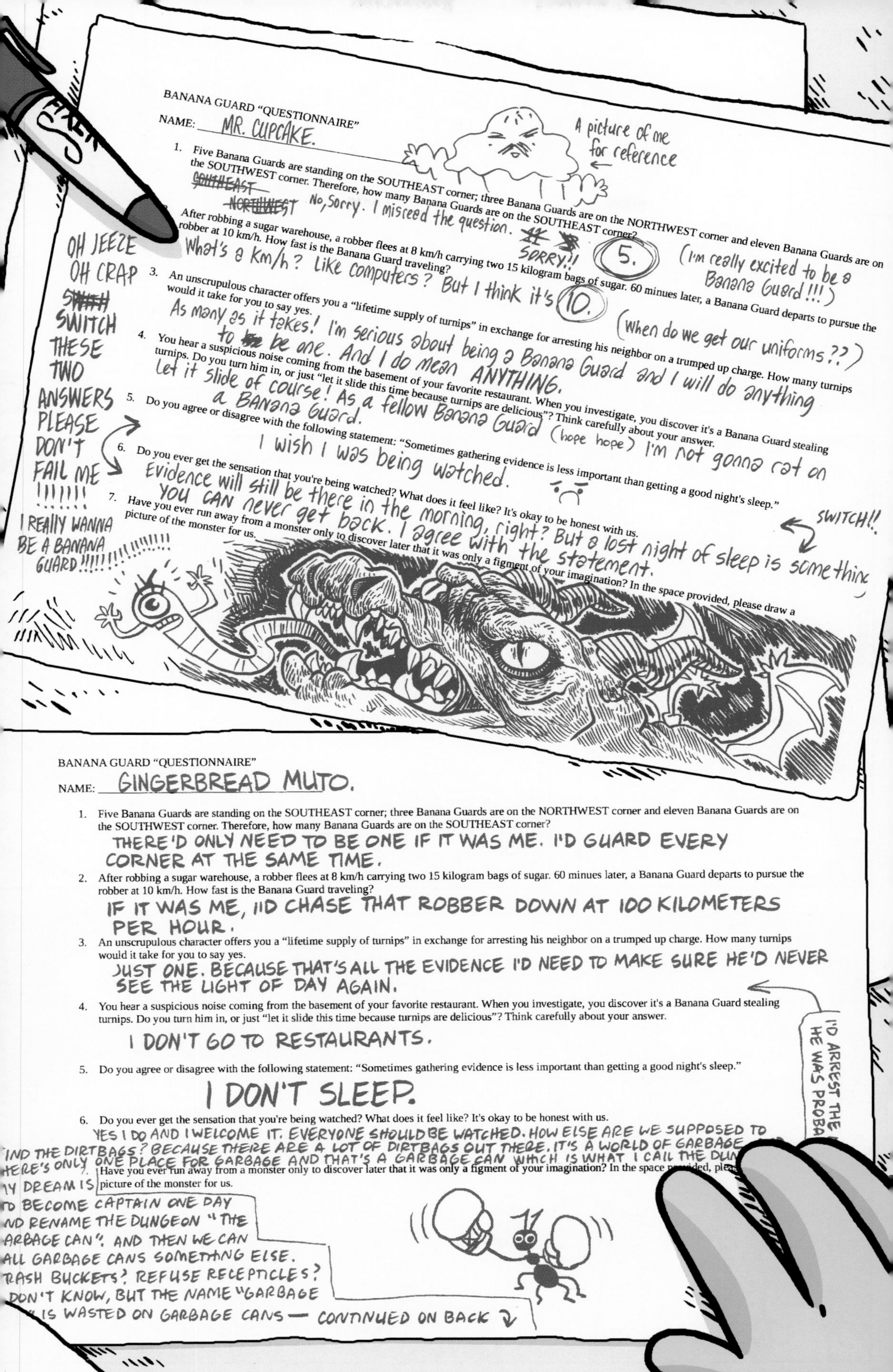

BANANA GUARD "QUESTIONNAIRE"
NAME: MR. CUPCAKE.
A picture of me for reference
1. Five Banana Guards are standing on the SOUTHEAST corner; three Banana Guards are on the NORTHWEST corner and eleven Banana Guards are on the SOUTHWEST corner. Therefore, how many Banana Guards are on the SOUTHEAST corner?
~~SOUTHEAST~~
~~NORTHWEST~~ No, Sorry. I misreed the question.
SORRY!! 5.
(I'm really excited to be a Banana Guard!!!)
2. After robbing a sugar warehouse, a robber flees at 8 km/h carrying two 15 kilogram bags of sugar. 60 minues later, a Banana Guard departs to pursue the robber at 10 km/h. How fast is the Banana Guard traveling?
What's a km/h? Like computers? But I think it's 10.
(When do we get our uniforms??)
OH JEEZE
OH CRAP
SWITCH THESE TWO ANSWERS PLEASE DON'T FAIL ME !!!!!!!
3. An unscrupulous character offers you a "lifetime supply of turnips" in exchange for arresting his neighbor on a trumped up charge. How many turnips would it take for you to say yes.
As many as it takes! I'm serious about being a Banana Guard and I will do anything to be one. And I do mean ANYTHING.
4. You hear a suspicious noise coming from the basement of your favorite restaurant. When you investigate, you discover it's a Banana Guard stealing turnips. Do you turn him in, or just "let it slide this time because turnips are delicious"? Think carefully about your answer.
Let it slide of course! As a fellow Banana Guard (hope hope) I'm not gonna rat on a Banana Guard.
5. Do you agree or disagree with the following statement: "Sometimes gathering evidence is less important than getting a good night's sleep."
Evidence will still be there in the morning, right? But a lost night of sleep is something you can never get back. I agree with the statement.
6. Do you ever get the sensation that you're being watched? What does it feel like? It's okay to be honest with us.
I wish I was being watched.
SWITCH!!
7. Have you ever run away from a monster only to discover later that it was only a figment of your imagination? In the space provided, please draw a picture of the monster for us.
I REALLY WANNA BE A BANANA GUARD!!!!!!!!!!!!
BANANA GUARD "QUESTIONNAIRE"
NAME: GINGERBREAD MUTO.
1. Five Banana Guards are standing on the SOUTHEAST corner; three Banana Guards are on the NORTHWEST corner and eleven Banana Guards are on the SOUTHWEST corner. Therefore, how many Banana Guards are on the SOUTHEAST corner?
THERE'D ONLY NEED TO BE ONE IF IT WAS ME. I'D GUARD EVERY CORNER AT THE SAME TIME.
2. After robbing a sugar warehouse, a robber flees at 8 km/h carrying two 15 kilogram bags of sugar. 60 minues later, a Banana Guard departs to pursue the robber at 10 km/h. How fast is the Banana Guard traveling?
IF IT WAS ME, I'D CHASE THAT ROBBER DOWN AT 100 KILOMETERS PER HOUR.
3. An unscrupulous character offers you a "lifetime supply of turnips" in exchange for arresting his neighbor on a trumped up charge. How many turnips would it take for you to say yes.
JUST ONE. BECAUSE THAT'S ALL THE EVIDENCE I'D NEED TO MAKE SURE HE'D NEVER SEE THE LIGHT OF DAY AGAIN.
I'D ARREST THE HE WAS PROBA
4. You hear a suspicious noise coming from the basement of your favorite restaurant. When you investigate, you discover it's a Banana Guard stealing turnips. Do you turn him in, or just "let it slide this time because turnips are delicious"? Think carefully about your answer.
I DON'T GO TO RESTAURANTS.
5. Do you agree or disagree with the following statement: "Sometimes gathering evidence is less important than getting a good night's sleep."
I DON'T SLEEP.
6. Do you ever get the sensation that you're being watched? What does it feel like? It's okay to be honest with us.
YES I DO AND I WELCOME IT. EVERYONE SHOULD BE WATCHED. HOW ELSE ARE WE SUPPOSED TO IND THE DIRTBAGS? BECAUSE THERE ARE A LOT OF DIRTBAGS OUT THERE. IT'S A WORLD OF GARBAGE HERE'S ONLY ONE PLACE FOR GARBAGE AND THAT'S A GARBAGE CAN WHICH IS WHAT I CALL THE DUN
7. Have you ever run away from a monster only to discover later that it was only a figment of your imagination? In the space provided, plea picture of the monster for us.
Y DREAM IS TO BECOME CAPTAIN ONE DAY ND RENAME THE DUNGEON "THE ARBAGE CAN". AND THEN WE CAN ALL GARBAGE CANS SOMETHING ELSE. RASH BUCKETS? REFUSE RECEPTICLES? DON'T KNOW, BUT THE NAME "GARBAGE IS WASTED ON GARBAGE CANS — CONTINUED ON BACK

GREAT GLOB! THESE TESTS ARE TERRIBLE!!!
WE SHOULD FAIL EACH AND EVERY ONE OF 'EM RIGHT NOW.
IN 'N' OUT
Oh, we can't do that sir.

WHAT?! WHY IN GLOBS NAME NOT?!
Princess Bubblegum's orders, sir.

She said we can't kick them out. They can only drop out.
Mmm.

WELL THEN... MAYBE WE SHOULD MAKE LIFE DIFFICULT FOR THEM.
MAYBE WE SHOULD TRAIN THEM SO HARD THAT THEY'LL BE BEGGING TO QUIT.
Sir, you get so angry when you look at that picture.

HE PRINCESS HAS NOTHING TO DO ITH THIS!
THE INTEGRITY OF THE GUARD IS AT STAKE.
DO YOU UNDERSTAND?!
Sir, yes sir!
CCREAKK
CLICK!
EVERYBODY UP!!!
BAM
KRASH

move it!
wee-ooh,
wee-ooh,
wee-ooh,
wee-ooh...
wee-ooh

If you're not back by sundown, you all have to sleep standing up!
10 MILE RUN

HUG ME
2 Miles 2 go

OoOhhh. I can't go on. And now we're all going to have to sleep standing up.

NOOO!

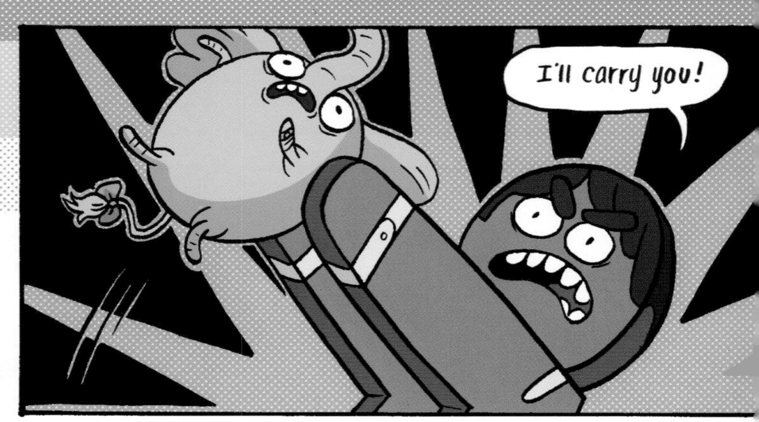
I'll carry you!

I'LL CARRY ALL OF YOU!

TUG
HAYYYYYY
GRUNT GRUNT
GRUNT GRUNT
this is very uncomfortable.
GRUNT GRUNT
CAN I HAVE SOME WATER?
I have to go to the bathroom.
MY LEG'S ASLEEP.
GRRRR!

Sir, they all finished!
FINISH
Before sundown!
IT'S BECAUSE OF THAT DANG GINGERBREAD MAN!
PAT PAT
I WANT YOU TWO TO *BREAK HIM.*
In half?!
WHAT? NO, BREAK HIS SPIRIT.
Ohhh.
heh heh.
Hey, Gingerbread. You got some more training to do.
NOTICE

Haw haw
Come on Cookie, you gonna run that slow when you're chasin' a perp?
Huff Puff

KACHUK
THUK
THUK
I hope you're not getting tired Cookie, because we're just warming up!
Ha haw
Huff Puff

THUK THUK
THUK
THUK
Sputter
sputter
die.

Uh... Where are we?
KSS SSS
I don't know. I think we're lost.

Lost?!

How are we gonna get back home?
GRRRR

Huff Puff huff
Did it work? Did we break you?
Yes. I'm exhausted.
Yes!
Mr. muto bread, We're all so tired, We can't go on.
Me... neither.
so then it's decided.
Yes. We all quit.
QUIT?!?
BUT I JUST GOT HERE!!!
Who are you?
I'M PUNCHY.
HERE, I GOT A NOTE FROM THE PRINCESS.
BOY IS IT GREAT TO BE HERE AND NOT IN JAIL.
Okay, it checks out.
Morning calisthenic in five minutes.

NOW, WHAT'S ALL THIS BOPPITY BIP ABOUT Y'ALL QUITTIN'?
we're terrible at this, Punchy.
WHAAAAAT?
BUT EVERYBODY'S GOOD AT SOMETHIN' RIGHT?
HOW 'BOUT YOU BRIGHT EYES, WHAT ARE YOU GOOD AT?
Handwriting analysis.
YOU SEE?
SHE'S GOOD AT HANDWRITING ANALYSIS!
WHAT ABOUT THE REST OF YOU GUYS?
Balancing things on my left hand!
Listening
HAVING VIVID DREAMS!
ROLLING AROUND.
Holding heavy objects.
baking apple pies.
remembering long lists.
TUG ME
i can make funny noises with my mouth.
DOING THINGS WITH my LEGS!
YOU SEE?

TSSSSSSS
Z
ADVENTURE TIME CHARACTER LIST
ABRACADANIEL
ANCIENT SLEEPING MAGI OF LIFE GIVING
BANANA MAN
BEARS
BILLY
BUFO
CANDY HEART CHEF
DUKE OF NUTS
JAKE JR.
JERMAINE
JOSHUA
THE LICH
NAKED WIZARD
OTHER LEMONGRAB
TREETRUNKS
TWO-HEADED DUCK

POKE
I KNEW YOU COULD DO IT!

NEXT : "A WELL-DESERVED" R'N'R

CHAPTER THREE
TUG ME

o, our cadets
re on R&R...
It's well-deserved, sir.
PERHAPS.
PERHAPS.
Yeah!
WOO HOO!
VROOM
BANANA GUARD
I'm gonna relax!
n gonna
ave so
ch rest!
BOTH FOR ME, THANKS!
This is a waste of time.
IT'S WELL-DESERVED.
that's why they call it 'r&r'.
WORLD OF BASEMENTS

BLAM
I Knew that tire looked over-inflated.
KA-BLAMO!
oh my gosh!
SO LOUD!
What was that?!
hm?
EEEEE
WOAH!
EEEERRRRR
FSSss
FSS
Uhhhh...

looks like we have a flat tire.
Sounded like it too!
Mm.
Mm.

i guess i can call princess bubblegum.
ohhh!
SO CAN I.

Beep
PEEBS.
CALL
Boop
Beep

BEMPP
NO SIGNAL

drat! no signal.
language! let's not resort to using the 'd' word!
NO SIGNAL?

OF COURSE THERE'S NO SIGNAL!

FOR THIS IS THE KINGDOM OF ICE!
wenk
wenk
wenk

SWOOosh
ding

...AND SNOW.
MOSTLY ICE THOUGH.
BUT YEAH, LOUSY RECEPTION.
WHAT CAN I DO FOR YA?

Oh mr. Ice King, can you help us with our bus? We're supposed to be restin' n' relaxin' from all our hard work at the banana guard academy.
BANANA GUARD ACADEMY?
YOU GUYS?
OH YEAH, I REMEMBER. I SAW IT ON THE NEWS I THINK.
BANANA GUARD ACADEMY #1
ANYWAYS, MY PENGUINS WILL HAVE YOU UP AND RUNNING IN NO TIME.
Oh thank you!
yay!
YOU ROCK ICE KING!
BANANA GUARD ACADEMY #1
IN THE MEANTIME, I'LL SHOW YOU TO YOUR ROOMS.
UH...
WAIT...
our rooms?
Ice King, there's been a misunderstanding.
We're headed to the jungle Kingdom.
THAT DUMP?
WHY NOT STAY IN MY Luxurious ICE HOTEL.
hm... it does look nice.
Ice hotels are cool!
THEN IT'S DECIDED.

Hey, i'm really moving up in the world!
the view is to die for!
Everything is ice!
CHECK OUT THESE PLUSH ROBES, YO!
CONCIERG
there's an ice gym!
ICE GYM!!
HOW MANY KEYS WOULD YOU LIKE?
One.
I'M IMPRESSED BY THE ARCHITECTURE.

ALL RIGHT YOU GUYS, I'M COUNTING ON YOU TO CATER TO OUR GUESTS' EACH AND EVERY WHIM.
ARE YOU LISTENING GUNTHER?

Wenk
"WENK." IT'S ALWAYS "WENK" WITH YOU.

SHOO
SHOO
SHOO
ALL RIGHT, WHAT ARE YOU WAITING FOR? GO! CATER!
Wenk
Wenk
Wenk

MR. MUTO BREAD, HOW IS EVERYTHING?
Fine.
NEED ANYTHING? AN EXTRA PILLOW?
No.
ARE YOU SURE?
Yes.

I'LL GET YOU AN EXTRA PILLOW.

LADY TRUNKS, EVERYTHING OKAY?
Yes, i'm just headed down to the ice sauna.
WHAT? ON FOOT? I'LL HAVE MY PENGUINS CARRY YOU.

Oh no that's all--
GUNTHER!

aaahhh!
500
500
CAN I DAB THE SWEAT FROM YOUR BROW?
WHAT? NO, I'M FINE.

NO PROBLEM AT ALL, SIR.
AHH! IT STINKS!

HOW'S THE FOOD?
DELICIOUS.
NEED ANY MUSTARD?
NO THANK YOU.

IT'S COMPLIMENTARY!
MY ICE CREAM!
PLORT

Haha
Wheee
?
SPROING
BOUNCE
BOING
BOUNCE BOING

NO NO NO.

SQUISH

SET DOWN

ALLOW ME.

BOUNCE
BOING
HA HA HA!
SPROING SPROING
WHEEE!
BOING

NEED ANYTHING?
SPLOOSH
aaahhhh!

uh... yeah, can you get me a club sandwich?
COMIN' UP.

pst. tree trunks. we gotta get outta here!

i don't know about you guys, but i cant rest or relax in this torture palace.
me neither.

wanna sneak out with--
YES
Yes!
Yep!
Yes!
yes
GLOB YES
YAS

Shh. Keep movin'
I don't have my suitcase.
We'll get new ones.
uh-oh
HEY, WHAT'S GOIN' ON?
SNEAK OUT ON ME, WILL YOU?!?
ZAP
ZAP
ZAP
ZAP
ZAP
GRRR RRRRRR
GUNTHER, SET UP THE GIANT CHESS BOARD!

HEE HEE, WATCH OUT GUNTER! I'M COMIN' AFTER YOUR ELEPHANT.

Wenk
WHAT'S HAPPENING? WHY CAN'T I MOVE?

I'm INSIDE MY OWN THOUGHTS...
IT'S SO PEACEFUL HERE.
IT'S KINDA WEIRD THAT I DON'T WANT TO PARTY.
ARE MY PARTY DAYS OVER? IS IT TIME FOR ME TO SETTLE DOWN?
Haha, now it's on wheels.
Boy, this is a comfy chair.

Lake Butterscotch? But I haven't been there in years...
The last time was with Wyatt...
I was so happy when I first met him...
But soon I couldn't wait to get away...
SUN
I guess you never completely forget the people who pass through your life...
GAH!!!
SPLAT
SUN
Hello?
They're always there in the back of your your mind...
Hmm.
I can see my house.

I like sitting on walls.
I like looking at my feet as they dangle over the ground.
It looks like i'm flying.
GRRRRRRRRRR!
I'm helpless
can't move
Stuck in place forever
my arms!
my legs!
my hands!
my hea
HGHHHRRRRR!
IF I PUSH A LITTLE HARDERRRR
why can't I break free?!

Ooo
WHEN WILL I BE A BANANA GUARD?
AS SOON AS I'M IN THE BANANA GUARD... I'M GONNA MARCH OVER TO HER HOUSE AND... UH...
OH JEEZ, I DON'T EVEN KNOW HER NAME...
AND IT WAS TEN YEARS AGO.
I NEVER STAYED IN TOUCH. I DON'T KNOW WHERE SHE LIVES! WHAT AM I--
breathe in... breathe out... remember your training...
remember your...

WOOOAAAAHHHH!
I can feeeel... Peppermint Butler
TRAINING
GAHHHH!!!...
@hhh!
Combining our powers!
Oh my! wha happening
COMBINING OUR DREAMS...

GRRRRRRRRR
EH?

KA-SHATTER
BOP!
AHHHH!

UHHH...

RUN!!!!!

Huff
Puff
Huff
Here he comes.
I HOPE THOSE PENGUINS FIXED THE BUS.
i've got a few tricks up my Sleeve.
We still have to climb on and drive away.
Yay! we made it!

enough ice King!
UHH!
B-ZAP!!

's over
e King.
it's over.
UHH
I JUST WANTED TO HELP YOU REST AND RELAX! SNIFF SNIFF
BUT YOU DID ICE KING!
Being frozen is very relaxing.
I feel reborn.
VROOOOOOM
You should try it!
Hmmmm
ZAP!

HM. WELL
THIS IS BORING.
I'M JUST
IN A BIG
EMPTY ROOM.
MAYBE IF I
FREEZE MYSELF.
ZAP
HM. STILL
BORING.
I KNOW!
ZAP
ZAP
ZAP
ZAP
ZAP

CHAPTER FOUR

HE MORNING AFTER R&R
HAVE THE NEW RECRUITS RETURNED FROM THEIR REST AND RELAXATION?
yes, commandant.
VERY GOOD. AND I ASSUME THEY RECIEVED *NEITHER*.
BANANA GUARD ACADEMY
T WITH THAT LAT TIRE WE ANGED... HEH HEH
IO'S *HUNGIE?*
Quite the opposite, sir.
EH?
Their rest and relaxation levels are off the charts.

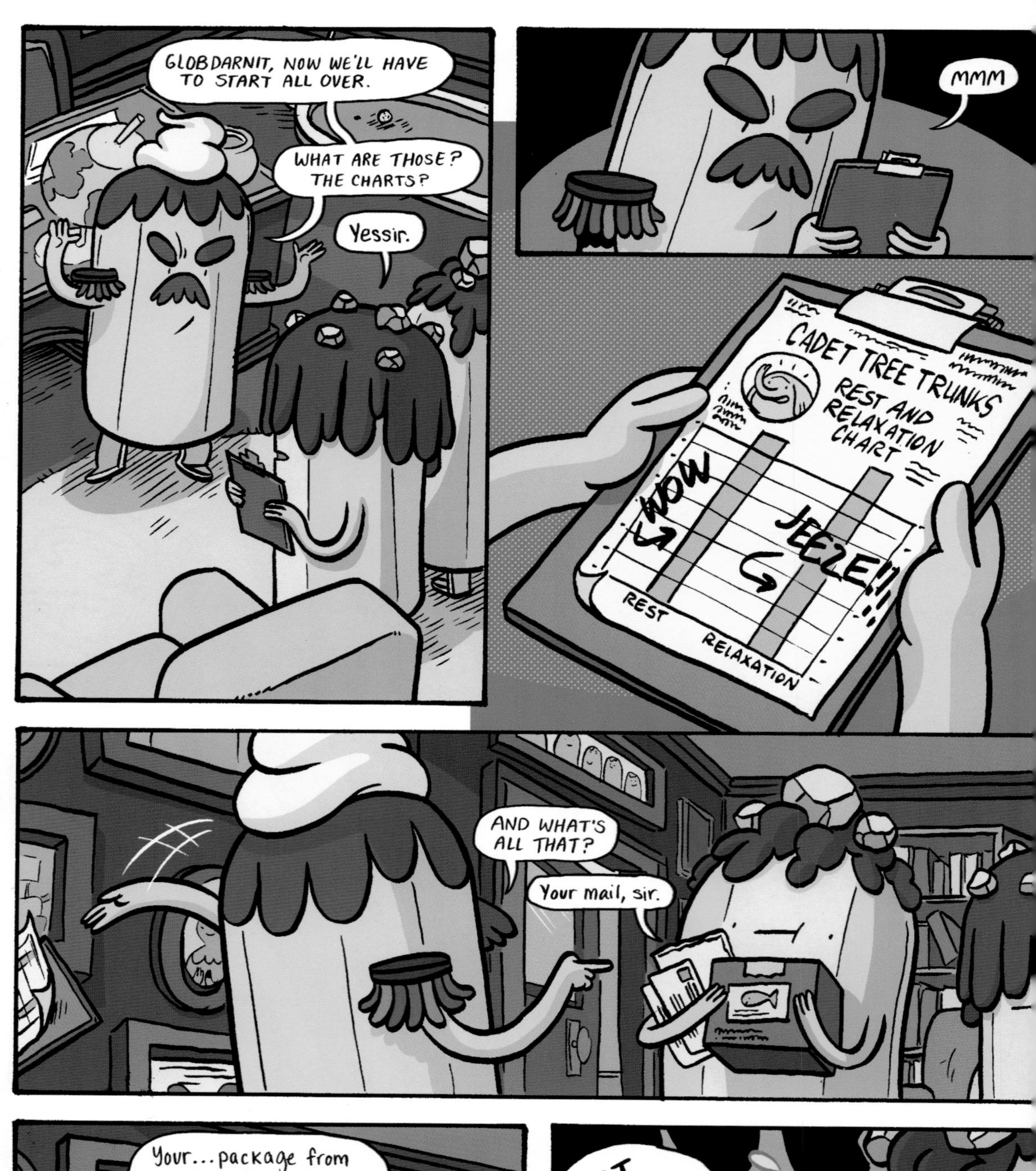
GLOBDARNIT, NOW WE'LL HAVE TO START ALL OVER.
WHAT ARE THOSE? THE CHARTS?
Yessir.
MMM
CADET TREE TRUNKS
REST AND RELAXATION CHART
WOW
JEEZE!!
REST
RELAXATION
AND WHAT'S ALL THAT?
Your mail, sir.

Your... package from "Robotic Fish Feeders Incorporated" finally arrived.
Snicker snicker

GET OUTTA HERE!!!

LAUGH AT SOMEONE FOR WANTING THINGS TO BE EASIER... GRUMBLE GRUMBLE

...LITTLE DO THOSE TWO NUMSKULLS KNOW, AS SOON AS I GET RID OF THE RECRUITS...

...I'LL BE GETTING RID OF THEM AS WELL! AHA HA HA HA!

AHA HAH HA
HA
HA

HA HA HA HA HA

AHH, I FELL SO RESTED AND RELAXED!
The rest of training is going to be a piece of cake.
I don't think we should be eatin' sweets, Mr. Muto Bread.
HOW ABOUT "EASY AS PIE?"
STOP YOU GUYS! YOU'RE MAKIN' ME HUNGRY!

WHAM!!
Hey cadets! We need to talk!
It's an emergency!

And why would we talk to you?
YEAH, WE KNOW WHAT YOU'VE BEEN UP TO.

Forget all that. We're on your side now.
The commandant hates us.
What do you think, Mr. Muto Bread?
Let's get the rest of the gang together for a jam session.
PLEASE STOP MENTIONING FOOD.

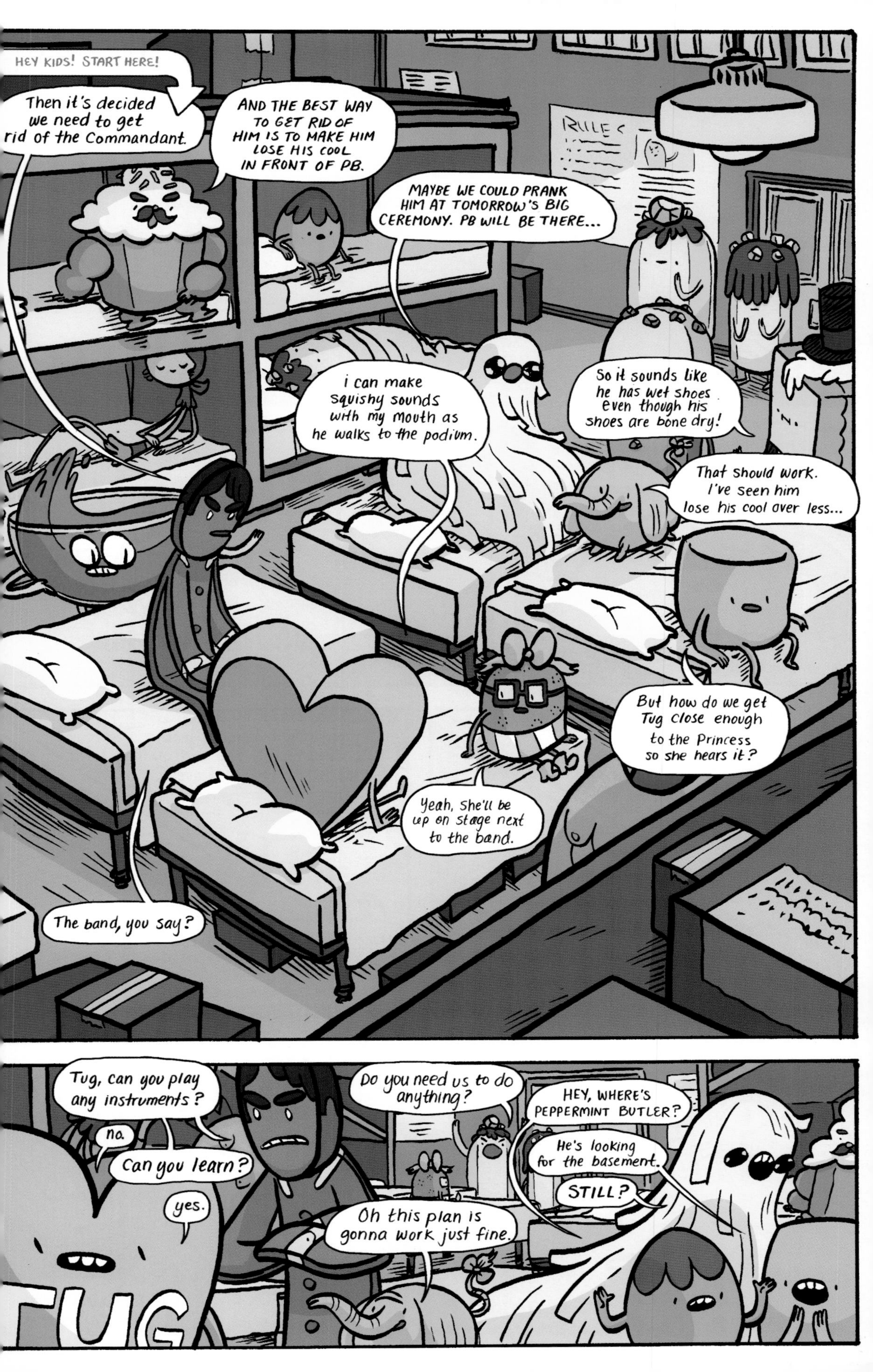
HEY KIDS! START HERE!
Then it's decided we need to get rid of the Commandant.
AND THE BEST WAY TO GET RID OF HIM IS TO MAKE HIM LOSE HIS COOL IN FRONT OF PB.
MAYBE WE COULD PRANK HIM AT TOMORROW'S BIG CEREMONY. PB WILL BE THERE...
i can make squishy sounds with my mouth as he walks to the podium.
So it sounds like he has wet shoes even though his shoes are bone dry!
That should work. I've seen him lose his cool over less...
But how do we get Tug close enough to the Princess so she hears it?
Yeah, she'll be up on stage next to the band.
The band, you say?
Tug, can you play any instruments?
no.
Can you learn?
yes.
Do you need us to do anything?
HEY, WHERE'S PEPPERMINT BUTLER?
He's looking for the basement.
STILL?
Oh this plan is gonna work just fine.
TUG

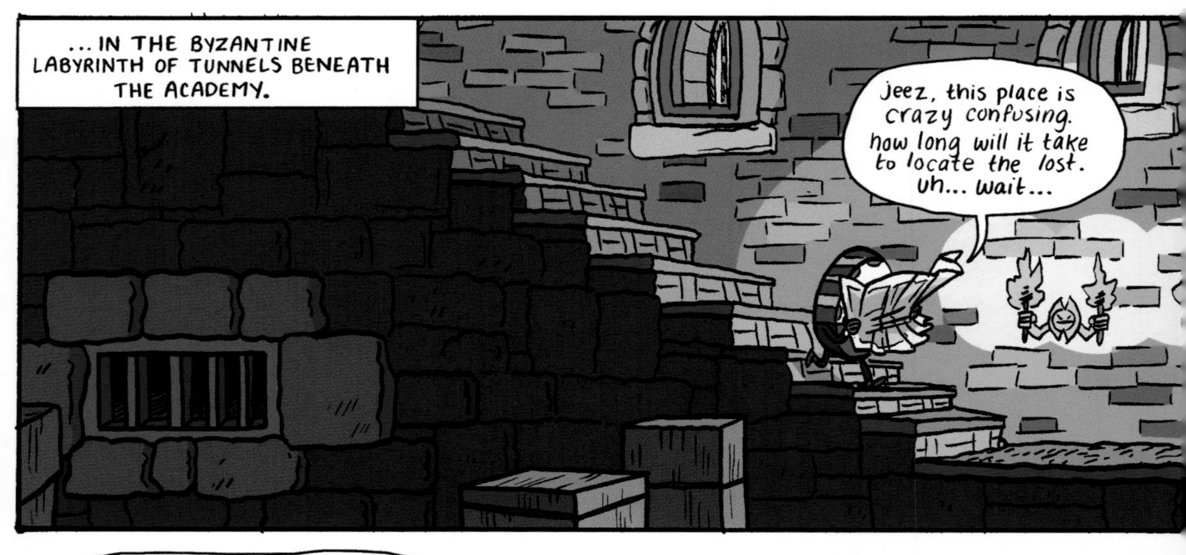

...IN THE BYZANTINE LABYRINTH OF TUNNELS BENEATH THE ACADEMY.
jeez, this place is crazy confusing. how long will it take to locate the lost. uh... wait...

...have i forgotten what it is i'm looking for? has it been that long?

PEP BUT'S SPECIAL RINGTONE FOR PRINCESS BUBBLEGUM

hi princess, how's it going? what can i do for you?
JUST WONDERING HOW THE COMMANDANT IS DOING?

commandant banana guard? he's... he's okay... he's still dealing with his issues, i guess.
OKAY. WELL KEEP ME POSTED IF HE DOESN'T WANT THE JOB THEN MAYBE I CAN REPLACE HIM WITH LEMONBLACK.

lemonblack? blech.
I KNOW RIGHT? HEY GOTTA RUN.

okay bye.
TAP
BYE.
TAP

strange. lemonblack was in my dream last night.

BACK IN THE BUNK ROOM
RULES
TUG ME
Oh Tug, it sounds wonderful!

This plan of yours is a blue ribbon winner Mr. Muto Bread. You're a natural leader.
Plan? what plan?
To get rid of the commandant.
What? why?
Because the Bananas told us he's trying to force us all to quit.
yeah but...haha... who cares? it'll never work. he's a banana. bananas are idiots.
RULES
i mean, no offense fellas.
Huh?
Hi Peppermint Butler!
Should i keep practicing?
Hmm

plus, PB told me that commandant's replacement will be lemonblack.
Lemonblack? Forget it, Tug. The plan's off.
oh dang.
Aw.
he was weird before that.
I've Been hearing disturbing stories about that dude. Ever since little Lemonhope escaped.
I think it's better to stick with the weirdo we know.
i agree.
Then it's decided. No pranks at the special ceremony.
that's showbiz.
Hey, where's Punchy?
He's having lunch with PB.
Again?
IN PRINCESS BUBBLEGUM'S PRIVATE LUNCHEON ROOM
HA HA, OH MAN, THIS IS BETTER THAN THE CRUD THEY SERVE AT THE ACADEMY. NOM NOM NOM...
OH PUNCHY.
MEK
BLOP
SCARF
SNURK
SO, HOW'S IT GOING OVER THE AT THE ACADEMY? ARE YOU TURNING YOUR LIFE AROUND

HUH? OH... YEAH I GUESS SO.
GOOD.
SCARF

OUR MAJESTY, THERE'S BEEN SOME SORT OF ACCIDENT AT CASTLE LEMONGRAB.
ACCIDENT?

YES... LEMONBLACK. HE... I'M GETTING REPORTS THAT HE... BLEW UP.
HA HA. WHAT?

YEAH, FROM WHAT I CAN TELL, LEMONHOPE RETURNED? AND PLAYED A HARP? OR SOMETHING. AND THEN LEMONBLACK EXPLODED! AND LEMONWHITE WAS IN HIS STOMACH AND NOW THERE'S BODY PARTS EVERYWHERE.
IT'S REALLY SOMETHING.

ALL RIGHT, I GUESS I'LL GO SEW HIM BACK TOGETHER.
SORRY PUNCHY, I GOTTA CUT OUR LUNCH SHORT.
NO PROBS. I'LL JUST TAKE THIS AND GO.
SWIPE

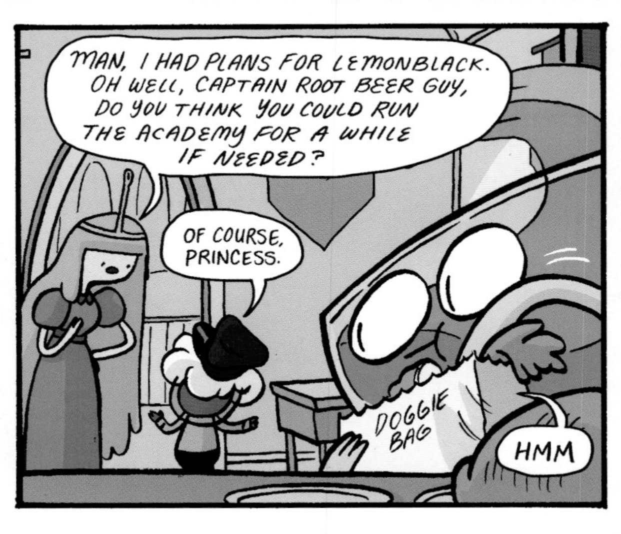
MAN, I HAD PLANS FOR LEMONBLACK. OH WELL, CAPTAIN ROOT BEER GUY, DO YOU THINK YOU COULD RUN THE ACADEMY FOR A WHILE IF NEEDED?
OF COURSE, PRINCESS.
DOGGIE BAG
HMM

BACK AT THE ACADEMY IMPORTANT LESSONS ARE BEING LEARNED.
wee-ooh
wee-ooh
Wee-ooh,
wee-ooh

BAM!
Hm?
BZZZZ
PUNCHY!
Okay, take five everybody. My phone says I gotta report to the precinct.
SO WHAT'S THE RUMPUS? WHY ISN'T TUG PRACTICING THE PICCOLO OR WHATEVER?
You didn't hear?
A
B
C

Turns out the replacement for the Commandant is that gas leak Lemonblack, So we stopped the plan.
WHAT? NO YOU GUYS, I WAS JUST WITH PB AND LEMONBLACK EXPLODED OR SOMETHING. HE'S GONNA BE IN REHAB FOR MONTHS. THE NEW REPLACEMENT IS ROOT BEER GUY.
Root Beer Guy?!
SALT OF THE EARTH!
A REAL LEADER!
He's awesome!
And super sweet!
HMM
All right Tug. The plan is back on! We gotta get rid of the commandant!
Yay!
oh man, i gotta re-learn what i've unlearned?
You'll be fine.
?
BZZ
TUG ME
hey you guys, i gotta run. something big is going on in the candy kingdom.

LATER
Oh Tug! It sounds so good. You're like sweet tea on a summer day. Haha, I should call you "Sweet T"!
Because your name starts with a T.
TUG ME
All right, that's enough. Now let's hear some of those squishy sounds.
Okay. Here goes.
squish-a squish-a
squish-a squish-a
Wait, are you sure this is gonna work?
Hmm...
WHAM!!
you guys! stop! change of plans!
WHAT? WHAT IS IT, PEPPERMINT BUTLER?
root beer guy.. is dead.
GASP!!!!...

THE FUNERAL OF CAPTAIN ROOT BEER GUY.
SOMETIMES, CANDY PEOPLE ARE SO SPECIAL THAT YOU CANNOT BRING THEM BACK.
ROOT BEER GUY
CAPTAIN ROOT BEER GUY WAS ONE OF THOSE SPECIAL PEOPLE.
So... now what?
DO WE GET RID OF THE COMMANDANT? OR KEEP HIM?
We could end up with someone better.
Or worse.
MAYBE WE SHOULD TALK ABOUT THIS LATER?
t this point I think 's safe to say that nyone could end up lacing the commandant.
Well we gotta do something!
TUG ME
SO WHY NOT ROLL THE DICE?
YOU'RE GAMBLING WITH OUR LIVES!
i've been practicing so hard!
I'm sensing some division among the group.

KEEP THE COMMANDANT!
?

DUMP THE COMMANDANT!

OKAY, SO IF TUG'S SQUISHY SOUNDS DON'T WORK, WHAT DO WE DO?
I've got a whole mess 'a whoopie cushions from my last bachelorette party.
HAHA PERFECT.
Wait, are they listening to us?
Can you hear what they're sayin'?
Yeah, something about whoopie cushions.
HAHA PERFEC
I'LL BRING A SHARP PIN.

RRRRRIIIINNGGG
I gotta go.
Yeah, me too.

MENU

meet me in the base- ment

MOMENTS LATER IN THE BASEMENT
Hey Gumdrop Lass, what's up?
Thanks for meeting me, Marshy.
Of course, we're friends.
Exactly.
Who cares if you wanna keep the commandant and I wanna dump him? We're friends.
Wait.
What?
I wanna dump him too.
What?!
Yeah, big time.
Well why were you sitting with the "Keep Him" Crowd?
Our table ran out of seats.
Well, what I said still stands. We're friends with everyone yet we're fighting because we can't agree.
It's a real bummerrrrrrrrrrr...

BUMMER...
BUMMER...
BUMMER
If only there was a way to know for sure which path to take.
that's it!
that's what I've been looking for! The lost Oracle of Pathaleses.
huh?
a truth sayer from an ancient dimensions. It can answer any "What should I do?" question.
it can answer this question.
the only risk is catastrophic structural damage to OUR dimension if we ask the question wrong.
...but the only way to get it wrong is if you show emotion while you ask the question!
come on! hee hee hee
SUGAR
helmets

EANWHILE
PEBBLES WANTS US TO PERFORM SECURITY DETAIL AT HER IMPORTANT CEREMONY.
COOL
HA HA OH MAN, LOOKS LIKE A MAJOR PRANK OFFENSIVE IS IN THE WORKS.
THIS IS GONNA BE GREAT!
whoopie
squish-a
squish-a
GREASE
JUG ME
BEDTIME STORIES FOR PIGS

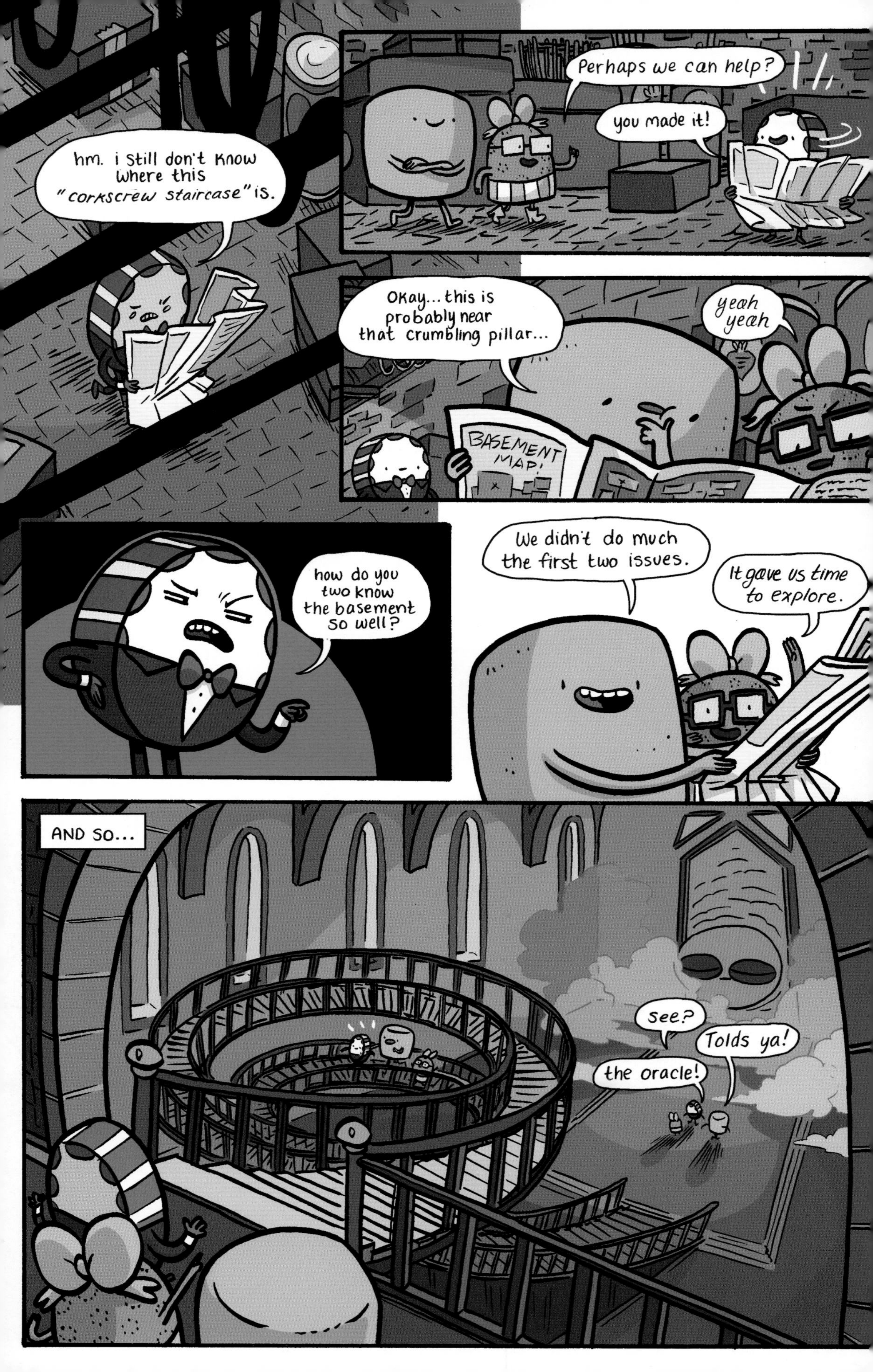
hm. i still don't know where this "corkscrew staircase" is.
Perhaps we can help?
you made it!
Okay... this is probably near that crumbling pillar...
yeah yeah
BASEMENT MAP!
how do you two know the basement so well?
We didn't do much the first two issues.
It gave us time to explore.
AND SO...
see?
Tolds ya!
the oracle!

hello! sorry to disturb you oracle, but i know you like "what should i do questions"
INDEED.
our master is focusing his energies n our destruction. We are unable to decide hether or not to get rid of him because his replacement might be worse. what should we do?
HMMM
THE ANSWER IS SIMPLE.
yes!
All right!
yeah!
YOU MUST...
HUH? WHAT'S THAT?
A FRACTURE IN THE PORTAL! THIS IS NOT GOOD!
CRACK!
KRKK!
I'M OUTTIE.

POP
RRRUUMMMBBELLLLEEEE

RIGHT AT THAT MOMENT
WOOSH!
POOOOT
woopie
BLARRRRPP
BLURPPP
POP!
Squish-a
squish-a
squisha
MUNCH
MUNCH
MUNCH
MUNCH
TOOOOT
woopie
"...AND SO THE LITTLE PIG YAWNED HIS BIGGEST YAWN AND SAID 'I'M SOOOOO TIRED!'..."
BEDTIME STORIES FOR PIGS
COMMANDANT...
You're...

ROOT
BEER
GUY

CHAPTER FIVE

COMMANDANT

YOU'RE

FIRRRRED!!!
...
POP!
Did ya see that? His moustache popped off.
WOW.
GUESS I'LL GO PACK MY THINGS.
e're too late.
She fired him.
The pranks worked.
TUG ME

LATER AT THE COMMANDANT'S HOUSE
MAYBE I'LL GET A JOB IN THE PRIVATE SECTOR.

So I guess thats it.
We'll never know if we made the right choice.
that's not what's worrying me.

i can't stop thinking about that fracture in the portal and what that means for this new timeline.

"new timeline"
What happened to the old one?
there is no old one.

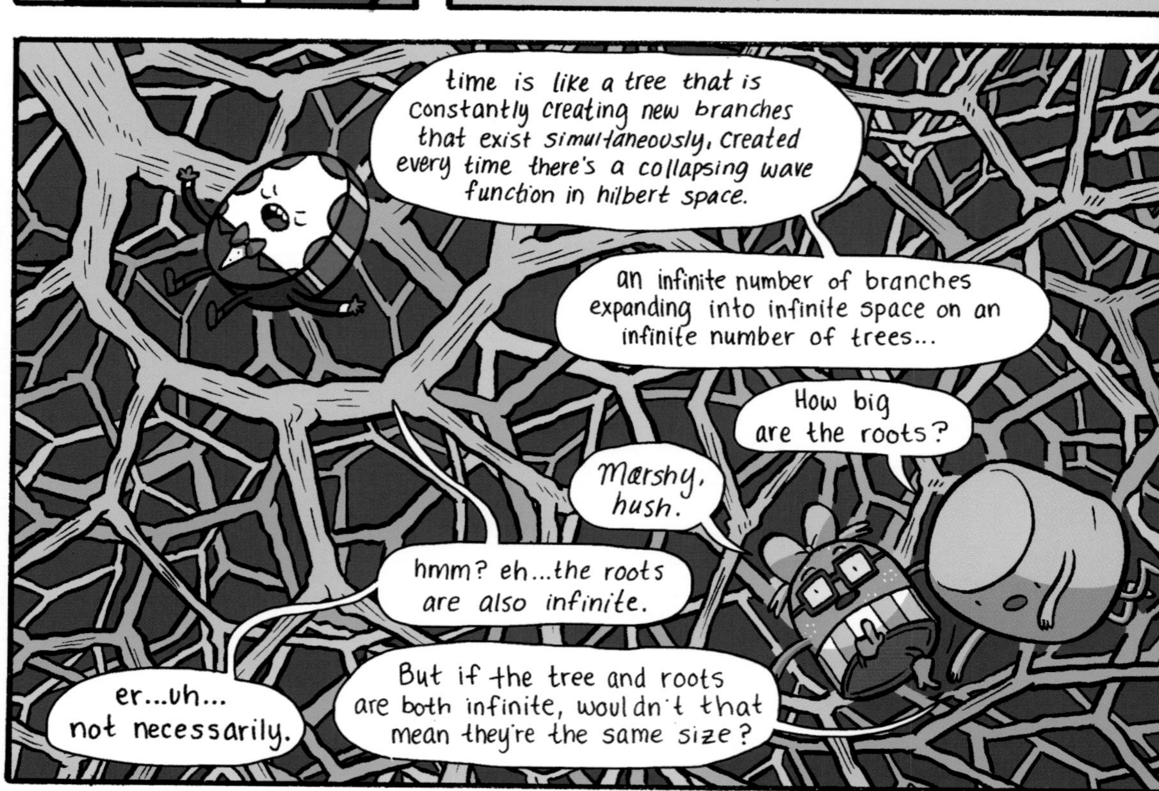
time is like a tree that is constantly creating new branches that exist simultaneously, created every time there's a collapsing wave function in hilbert space.
an infinite number of branches expanding into infinite space on an infinite number of trees...
How big are the roots?
Marshy, hush.
hmm? eh...the roots are also infinite.
But if the tree and roots are both infinite, wouldn't that mean they're the same size?
er...uh... not necessarily.

...but when there's a fracture, the branches can become entwined and disrupt the delicate balance of the multiverse...
...Causing the whole thing to collapse like a house of cards!
oh no!
So... hang on...is it a tree or a house of cards?
WOULD YOU GET OUT OF HERE?! I JUST GOT FIRED!!
FLEE!
AND MY MOUSTACHE POPPED OFF!
we have to get as close as we can to the energies of the other us's.
THE ONES FROM THE OTHER TIMELINE WHERE THE COMMANDANT WAS NOT FIRED.
hmm, if he hadn't been fired, he'd probably be celebrating.
At the Officer's Club.
let's go!

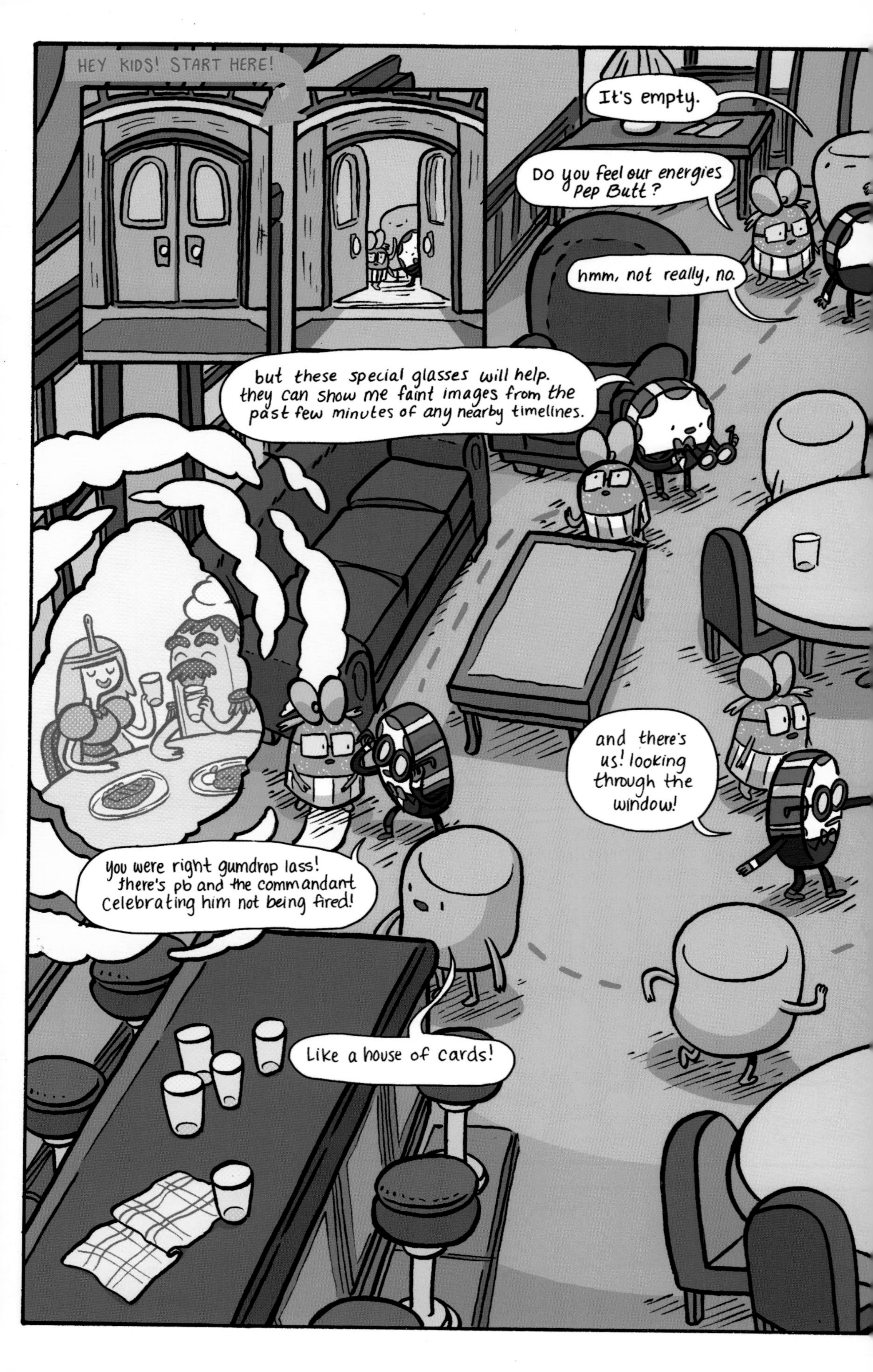
HEY KIDS! START HERE!
It's empty.
Do you feel our energies Pep Butt?
hmm, not really, no.
but these special glasses will help. they can show me faint images from the past few minutes of any nearby timelines.
you were right gumdrop lass! there's pb and the commandant celebrating him not being fired!
and there's us! looking through the window!
Like a house of cards!

and now we're running away, presumably to find the energies of us in this timeline!
so, right now the other us's are at the commandants realizing that we're here!
we should meet at the halfway point between here and there!
GOOD JOB! TURN THE PAGE!

(THE HALFWAY POINT BETWEEN HERE AND THERE)
YOU FOUND ME!
CAPTAIN ROOT BEER GUY?!
YES, IT IS I, CAPTAIN ROOT BEER GUY, APPEARING TO YOU IN SPIRIT FORM!
of course! your recent passing allowed your energy to use the fracture portal to visit us.
Sorry you died, dude.
Yeah, that Maja is a real wad.
SHE'S GOT SOME ISSUES.
So... wait, are our other energies here?
YEAH THEY'RE RIGHT OVER THERE ... IN FACT... HOLD ON A SEC.
BOOP!

CAW
mm... well i guess we'll just wait until he comes back.
Hey Peppermint Butler, do you ever wonder if we're all really robots?
huh? whaddya mean, marshy?
Like, what if we're robots and we don't even know it because we've been PROGRAMMED to think we're candy?
that seems like a tremendous waste of resources to me. far easier for robots to simply run a simulation of candy people who think they're real. that way you don't have to make all those robots.
Ohhhhhhh!
Oh boy. marshy. come on.
BOOOOOP!
I'M BACK!

HEY, YOU GUYS WEREN'T JUST TALKIN' ABOUT ROBOTS, WERE YA?

uh... no not really. We were talking about simulation theory mostly.
UH... OKAY.

OKAY, SO LOOK, BY NOW I'M SURE YOU'VE REALIZED THE FRACTURE HAS CAUSED THESE TWO TIMELINES TO BECOME ENTWINED...

...AND THAT COULD MUCK UP THE ENTIRE MULTIVERSE.
yes.
We figured it out right away.
no one els
has thoug

FLIP
FLIP
OKAY GOOD, SO LET'S SEE... ACCORDING TO THIS, ALL YOU HAVE TO DO... IS...

wait. what's that?
HUH?
what is that? What are you reading from?

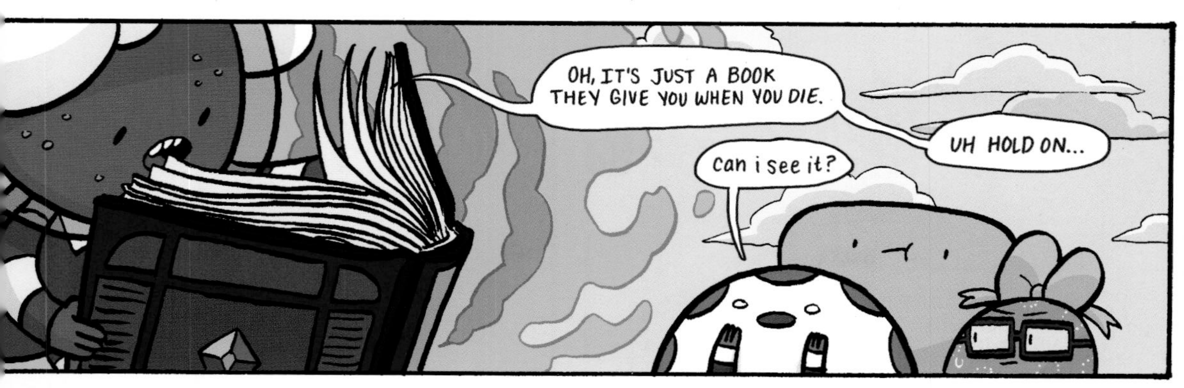
OH, IT'S JUST A BOOK THEY GIVE YOU WHEN YOU DIE.
UH HOLD ON...
can i see it?

HEY! HE WANTS TO KNOW IF HE CAN SEE IT!
...
PEPPERMINT BUTLER.

UH... NO, HE'S WITH TWO CANDY KIDS...
...
OKAY.

SORRY, MAYBE SOME OTHER TIME.
aw man.

OKAY, SO LOOK. YOU KNOW THAT GREY GOO THAT WAS OOZIN' OUT OF THAT FRACTURE?
yeah...
Y'ALL GOTTA EAT IT.

what?!
THAT'S IT, THAT ALL YA GOTTA DO. AND IF THE OTHER YOU'S EAT IT AT THE SAME TIME, THE TIMELINES WILL RE-MERGE.
And the multiverse will be saved!
Like a house of cards!

BLOO
ALL RIGHT, GOTTA RUN. BUT I'M SURE I'LL SEE Y'ALL AGAIN DOWN THE ROAD.

OOOP!
hmm.

Peppermint Butler?
yeah?
Do you think the other US's are walking up to the fracture right now? AT THE SAME TIME?
yeah probably. i hope so.
Ugh. all right. let's do this.

NOM NOM NOM NOM
Tastes like cold mashed potatoes.
blech
For the multiverse!

Well...
...let's hope this works!
Mm
hurk

REVIOUSLY IN BANANA GUARD ACADEMY

LATER AT THE OFFICER'S CLUB.
OF COURSE I KNEW THERE WERE GOING TO BE PRANKS, AND I SAID TO MYSELF, "BERNARD, LET THEM HAVE THEIR FUN! AM I SO FAR REMOVED FROM THE CALLOWNESS OF MY OWN YOUTH?"

So thats that I guess.
The right choice... we'll never know.
that's not what's bothering me.

the fracture in the portal and what it means for this new timeline is what i can't stop thinking about.

"New" timeline?
What happened to the old one?
there is no old one.

time is like a cracked windshield that is constantly creating new cracks that exist simultaneously, created every time there's a collapsing wave function in hilbert space.
an infinitely large windshield containing an infinity of cracks stretching into infinity.
How big's the car?
Marshy, hush.
hmm? eh... the car is also infinite.
But if the car and windshield are both infinite, wouldn't that mean they're the same size?
er... uh... not necessarily.

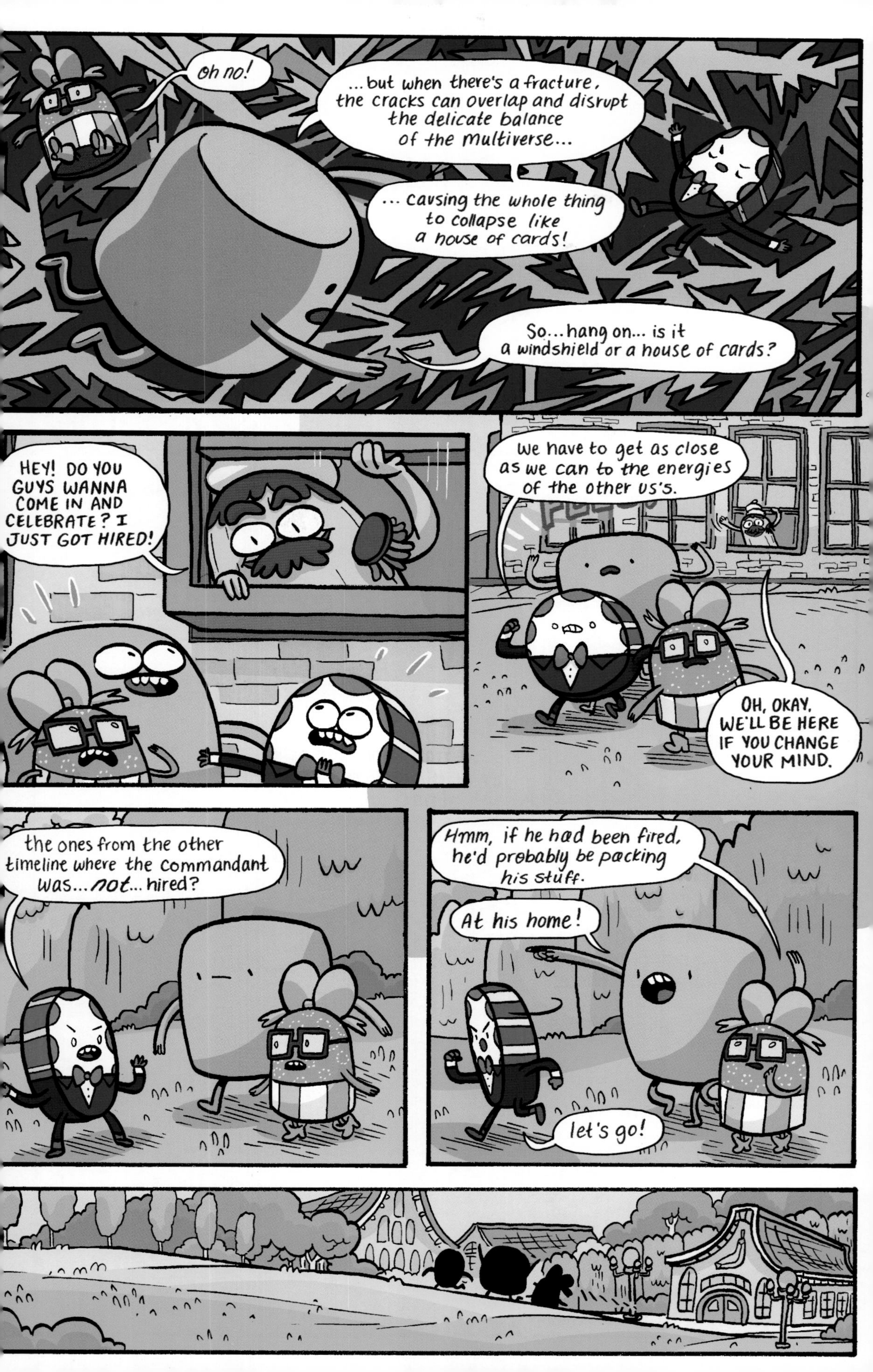
oh no!
...but when there's a fracture, the cracks can overlap and disrupt the delicate balance of the multiverse...
... causing the whole thing to collapse like a house of cards!
So...hang on... is it a windshield or a house of cards?
HEY! DO YOU GUYS WANNA COME IN AND CELEBRATE? I JUST GOT HIRED!
We have to get as close as we can to the energies of the other us's.
OH, OKAY, WE'LL BE HERE IF YOU CHANGE YOUR MIND.
the ones from the other timeline where the commandant was...not...hired?
Hmm, if he had been fired, he'd probably be packing his stuff.
At his home!
let's go!

and now we're running away, presumably to find the energies of us in this timeline!
so, right now the other us's are at the officer's club realizing that we're here!
we should meet at the halfway point between here and there!
AT THE COMMANDANT'S APARTMENT

HEY KIDS! START HERE!
It's empty.
Do you feel our energies Pep Butt?
hmm, not really, no.
but these special glasses will help. they can show me faint images from the past few minutes of any nearby timelines.
you were right gumdrop lass! there's pb and the commandant packing his things!
and there's us! looking through the window!
Like a house of cards!
GOOD JOB! TURN THE PAGE!

(THE HALFWAY POINT BETWEEN THERE AND HERE)
CAW
this is it, right?
yeah, they should be right in front of us.
well maybe we're a little early.
why dont you put on your special glasses?
huh? oh yeah.
Hey Peppermint Butler, do you ever wonder if we're all really robots?
huh?

YOU FOUND ME!
CAPTAIN ROOT BEER GUY?
HA HA ISN'T THAT SOMETHING? ANYWAY, I DON'T HAVE A LOT OF TIME, THE OTHER YOU'S ARE RIGHT OVER THERE.
THE LONG AND SHORT OF IT IS, I NEED Y'ALL TO EAT THE GREY GOOP FROM THE FRACTURE.
Eat it?
Blech
will that re-merge the timelines?
YEAH... OH, WAIT. ONE IMPORTANT THING: Y'ALL WEREN'T JUST TALKING ABOUT ROBOTS WERE YA?
erm... uht... no, not really.
OKAY GOOD! HOLD TIGHT, LEMME JUST CHECK ON THE OTHER YOU'S. BACK IN A JIFF!
SHUT
BOOP!

did you see that book he was reading from?
what was up with that?

Peppermint Butler, he asked if we were talkin' about robots and you said, "not really" but we kind of were...
hm? oh, it's fine. just a procedural formality.

i wouldn't worry about it. if our talking about robots really were an issue, they wouldn't send some noob spirit with a book to warn us.

who wouldn't send some noob spirit with a book?
huh? i don't know. whoever printed the book in the first place.

i mean, right? what's with the book? seems like we're dealing with some intergalactic cosmic bureaucracy and they're worried that we're chatting about robots?

is he reading from the same book?
and what's he doing now? talking to the other us's?
and is the other me asking about that book?
'cuz that's what i'd do. i mean the other me would... i...
jeez, this is really confusing me-- i mean him... i mean me!

BLOOOOP!
Look!
I'M BACK!
YAHH!
OKAY, THEY WEREN'T TALKING ABOUT ROBOTS EITHER, ITS ALL GOOD. GO TO THE FRACTURE RIGHT NOW, EAT THE GOOP AND EVERYTHING WILL BE FINE!
BUT YOU GOTTA GO! RIGHT NOW!
NOM NOM
So gross!
House of cards... robots... mashed potatoes.
For the multiverse!
well...
... let's hope this works.
mm
hurk

well, let's hope this works!
let's hope this works!
let's hope this works!
let's hope this works!
let's hope this works!
let's hope this works!
let's hope this works!
let's hope this works!
MMANDANT
YOU'RE...
I QUIT!!
GETTING TOO OLD FOR THIS...

ALL RIGHT EVERYBODY, ONLY ONE WEEK UNTIL GRADUATION!
We did it!
The timelines merged!
Bye Commandant!
TUG

But Peppermint Butler, aren't you worried about that robot stuff?
Yeah, what was that about?

it's probably fine.

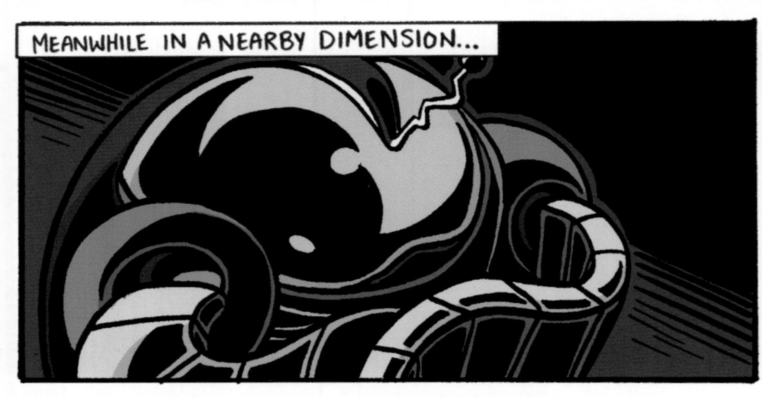
MEANWHILE IN A NEARBY DIMENSION...

BEEP

MUST... KILL... EVERYTHING...
...IN OOO!

CHAPTER SIX
TUG
ME

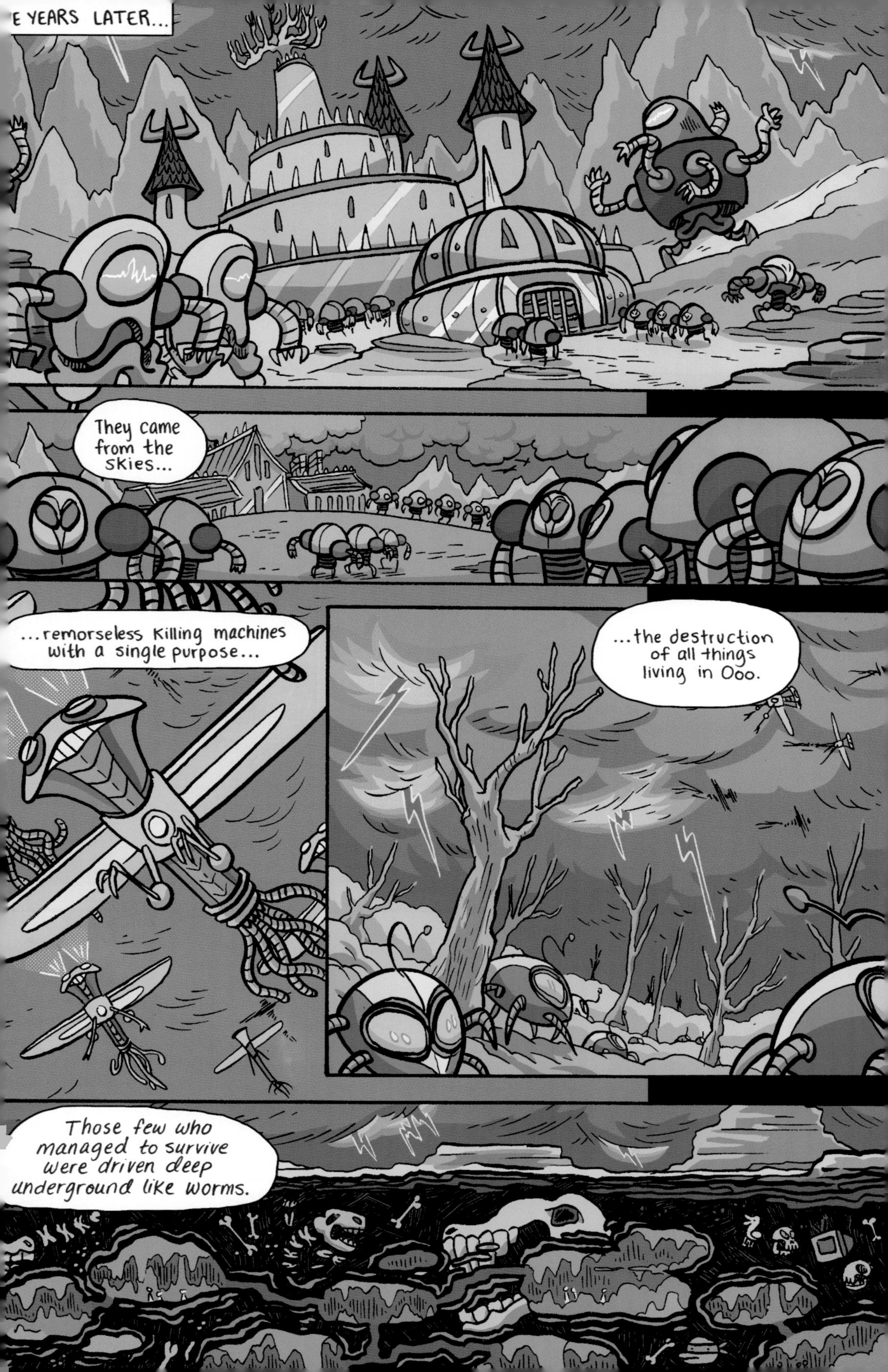

E YEARS LATER...
They came from the skies...
...remorseless killing machines with a single purpose...
...the destruction of all things living in Ooo.
Those few who managed to survive were driven deep underground like worms.

Their only sustenance, a revolting slurry of cave mold and old bones.
They called it slime-bone st
It's taste was so disgustin
many claimed to prefer the ta
of their own throw-up to--
CUT IT OUT.
IT'S HARD ENOUGH TO EAT THIS STUFF WITHOUT YOU JIBBER JABBERING IN MY EAR ALL THE TIME!
BAP!
The princess had grown weary of the jibber jabbering in her ears.
She was sick to death of the two Church of Root Beer Guy acolytes.

Forever narrating her sad tale for all to hear.
As our Lord Root Beer Guy himself had once done in previous issues.
BGA ISSUE #1

RUHHH! Make them stop!
Princess Bubblegum pounded her fists on the table.
She was past her breaking point.

ALL RIGHT YOU TWO, GIVE IT A REST FOR A WHILE.
As yo
comma
my Lo

I GOTTA ADMIT, HAVING MY OWN ACOLYTES IS A REAL HOOT.
YESSIR. A REAL HOOT.

HEY DUDES! PUT DOWN YOUR SLIME SPOONS, YOU'RE NOT GONNA BELIEVE THIS!
HIS IS IT! THIS IS WHAT WE'VE BEEN WAITING FOR!

Is it apples? Please oh please say it's apples.

HEH HEH. IT'S WAY BETTER THAN APPLES, TREE TRUNKS.

Better than apples?

IMPOSSIBLE!! Nothing is better than apples.
BAM
BAM

H YEAH?
T EVEN...

... THIS?!
Hello everyone.

I DON'T GET IT.

BMO'S BEEN WORKING DEEP COVER FOR ME AND JAKE SINCE THIS WHOLE ROBOT APOCALYPSE JAZZ STARTED.
BUT THIS IS THE FIRST TIME HE'S GOTTEN US SOLID INTEL WE CAN USE!

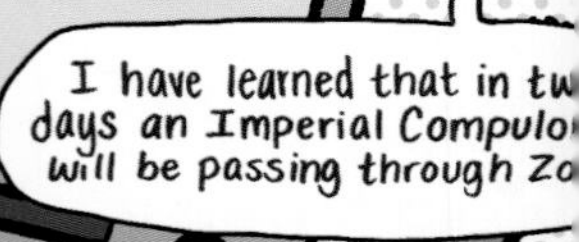
You are very right abo
that Finn and Jake
I have learned that in tw
days an Imperial Compulo
will be passing through Zo

And we can bake this Compulord in a delicious pie?!

A COMPULORD IS A KIND OF ROBOT.
BLECCCH!
Robot pie? How dreadful!
I'LL DIE BEFORE A SINGLE CRUMB OF ROBOT PIE PASSES THESE LIPS!!!

no no no, don't you see? imperial compulords are fully integrated into the robot datacore!
WHICH MEANS IF WE CAN KIDNAP AND INTERROGATE ONE...
WE CAN LEARN HOW TO DEFEAT THEM!

AND THE GOOD NEWS IS THOSE IMPERIAL COMPU-JERKS ARE ALL A BUNCH OF WIMPS.
HE WON'T STAND A CHANCE AGAINST THESE MEAT WEAPONS.

NE-M. TWO DAYS LATER.
sigh.
THIS VIEW PLEASES US NOT.

Make it better.

Uh...
You want us to change the... view?

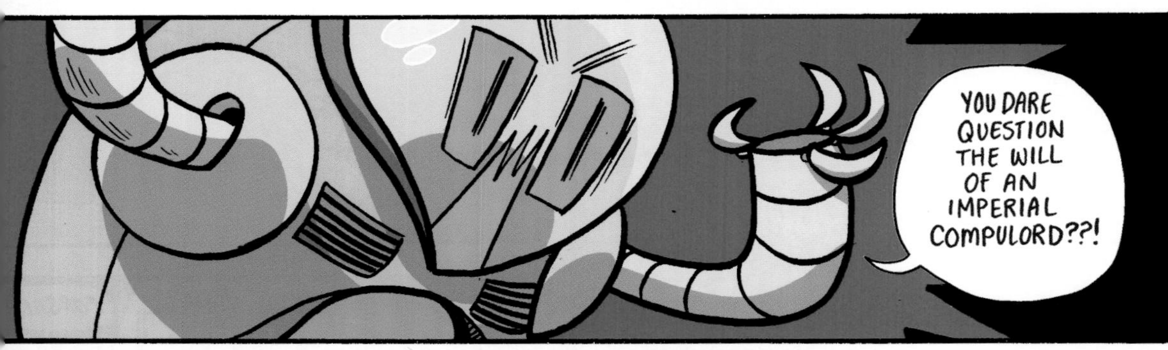
YOU DARE QUESTION THE WILL OF AN IMPERIAL COMPULORD??!

n-n-n-no Exalted one.
It shall be done.

THIS INFERAL RACKET WILL BE THE DEATH OF US!
b-b-but you s-s-said to ch-ch-change the v-v-view, exalted one!
CLANK
CLANK
CLANG
VRRRRRR
BOO
VRRRRR
CLANG

YOU FOOLS! WE ARE DISPLEASED! WE ARE MOST DISPLEASED!
WE CAN'T STAND THE SIGHT OF YOU! SELF-DESTRUCT YOURSELVES AT ONCE! ALL OF YOU!

even us?
ALL OF YOU!!!
AT ONCE!!!

BOOM
BOOM
BOOM
BOOM
BOOM
BOOM
BOOM
BOOM
BOOM

POP!
WE ARE... ALONE.

FORSAKE

It is like clockwork. Every ninety-three minutes he makes them blow up.

It will take four minutes for his replacements to arrive.
C'MON! WHAT ARE WE WAITING FOR?!
NOT HERE, YO.
IT'S TOO OUT IN THE OPEN.
Observe. His route passes through the Valley of Fissures.
VALLEY OF FISSURES...
Here is where he will blow up his servants.
RIGHT AT THE BOTTOM OF A FISSURE.
Yes. Yes I see.
Because the bottom of a fissure would be an ideal place for...

... an abduction.

THIS GUY GETS IT.
grrrr
grrrr

LATER. THE VALLEY OF FISSURES.
IMPUDENT KNAVE! WE ASKED FOR OIL, NOT THIS WRETCHED TUB OF GOOP YOU SET BEFORE US!
Apologies, Excellency! We--
SILENCE!
WAIT FOR IT...
THIS IS INTOLERABLE!!!
BOOM
BOOM
BOOM
BOOM
BOOM
BOOM
NOW!!!
AH, THE NEW SERVANTS, AT LONG LAST. WERE YOU GOING TO KEEP US WAITING HERE ALL DAY?
WHAT MANNER OF MACHINES ART THOU? YOUR BODY COVERINGS ARE UNFAMILIAR TO US. IS THIS SOME NEW FORM OF SYNTHETIC EXO-FLESH?
YOU. DRAW NEAR SO THAT WE MIGHT INSPECT THEE.

YES. WE LIKE IT WELL.
WE WILL HAVE IT.
REMOVE THIS ONE'S FLESH FOR US.
SHRUG
NOBODY'S REMOVIN' NOTHIN'!
YEAH! 'CAUSE THIS EXO-FLESH AIN'T SYNTHETIC!
IT'S ALL REAL, BABY.
WHA???
BUT...IT CAN'T BE! YOUR KIND ARE ALL... DEAD.
GUARDS! SEIZE THEM!
GUARDS?

PLEASE! NO MORE! WE CAN'T STAND IT!
OOOOHHHHH! THE AGONY.
NOBODY'S EVEN TOUCHED YOU, YOU BIG BABY!

THIS CHAIR IS SO HARD...
...SO VERY HARD UPON OUR EXALTED POSTERIOR.
WE HAVE NEVER KNOWN SUCH SUFFERING.

PLEASE, WE BEG YOU. EVEN THE THINNEST OF CUSHIONS WOULD NOT GO AMISS.
ANYTHING TO RELIEVE THIS CRUSHING BURDEN YOU HAVE PLACED UPON OUR ROYAL CHEEKS.
I DON'T GET WHY THEY WOULD PUT SENSORS IN YOUR BUTT CHEEKS TO BEGIN WITH.

MAY A COMPULORE NOT KNOW THE HUMBLE PLEASURES OF A CUSHION'S SOFT EMBRACE.

YOU WANT A CUSHION?
SURE, NO PROBLEM. YOU CAN HAVE A CUSHION...
...AS SOON AS YOU START TALKIN'!

ALL RIGHT! YOU WIN!
WE WILL TELL YOU ANYTHING! JUST MAKE IT STOP!
VERY WELL.

PEPPERMINT BUTLER. A CUSHION FOR OUR EXALATED GUEST.
right away, m' lady.

SCAMPER
SCAMPER

HE SHOULD BE BACK ANY MINUTE.

H, WHILE WE HAVE YOU...
'VE BEEN MEANING TO ASK.
WHY DID YOU GUYS INVADE US, ANYWAY?

WHY?
YOU MEAN...YOU DON'T KNOW?
I'M ASKIN' AIN'T I?

WE WERE SUMMONED, OF COURSE.
SUMMONED? BY WHO?

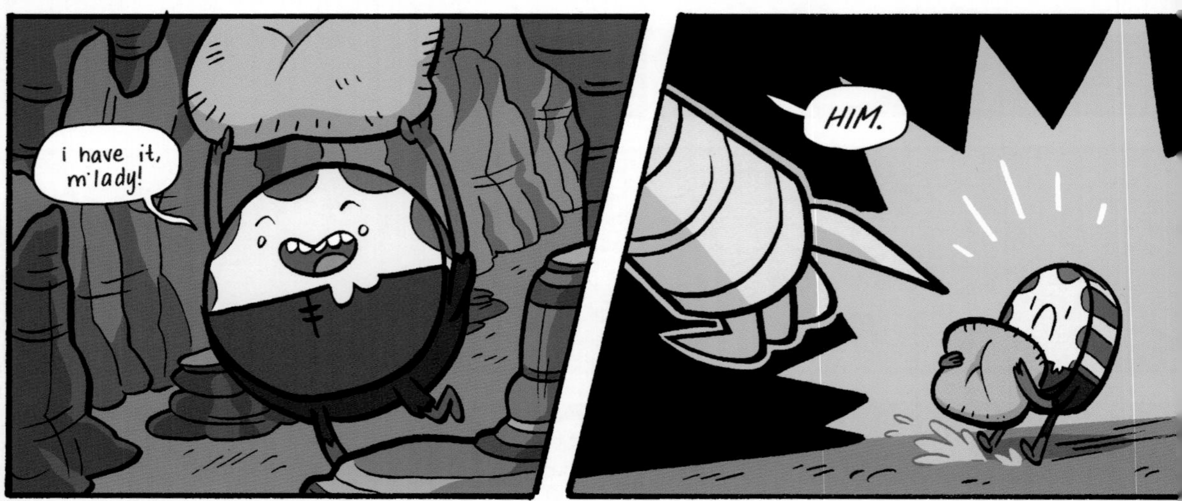
i have it, m'lady!
HIM.

i did what now?

oh, it's true! but how was i to know a little harmless banter about robots would bring about all this?

to be fair, root beer guy could've been a teeny bit more forthcoming about what would happen.

ROOT BEER GUY
ME? HOW AM I TO BLAME? I ASKED YOU WHETHER OR NOT YOU WERE TALKING ABOUT ROBOTS AND YOU SAID NO.
WHAT WAS I SUPPOSED TO DO? CALL YOU A LIAR?
RGIVE A RESTLESS OLD IOST FOR BEING NAIVE NOUGH TO ASSUME HIS FRIENDS AREN'T LYING TO HIM.
THE CRUEL TWIST OF FATE IN ALL THIS IS, IF YOU'D ONLY TOLD THE TRUTH IT WOULD'VE BEEN SUCH AN EASY FIX...
UH-HUH, HERE IT IS... PAGE 148...
"IF ROBOT YOU INVOKE, THEN FIVE TIMES 'CANCEL CANCEL CANCEL' MUST BE SPOKE."
five times 'cancel cancel cancel' so... you have to say 'cancel' fifteen times in other words.
HMM... NO. WELL, YES. TECHNICALLY. BUT WHAT I THINK THEY'RE GOING FOR IS FIVE GROUPINGS OF THREE WITH A BRIEF PAUSE BETWEEN EACH GROUPING TO SET THEM APART FROM EACH OTHER.
SO YOU'D GO... 'CANCEL CANCEL ANCEL'...PAUSE...'CANCEL CANCEL CANCEL... PAUSE... FIVE TIMES IN A ROW.
ah, i see!
what if you went 'cancel cancel' and then something got caught in your throat before you said the third one? would the whole thing re-set? OR would it remember where you were?
i guess what i'm asking is would you have to start over?
... IT DOESN'T REALLY SAY...

CANCEL CANCEL CANCEL!...
CANCEL CANCEL CANCEL!...
CANCEL CANCEL CANCEL!...
CANCEL CANCEL CANCEL!...
CANCEL CANCEL CANCEL!...

YEAH, KINDA ONE OF THOSE DEALS WHERE YOU GOTTA DO IT *BEFORE* THE ROBOTS GET HERE.

IT WAS ITS OWN REWARD.

YEAH!!
Go Finn and Jake! Go!
And so the two old friends hi-fived once more.
As they had done so many times in the past.

It truly was the very best of times.

The end.

THE END

Of course the ending of one thing...
...is merely the start of something else.
But would that something else be wonderful?
Or Hooooorrrrrrrifying?
Only time would tell--
FOR FUDGE'S SAKE! KNOCK IT OFF!
WOAH! LANGUAGE!
E'RE IN CHURCH.
oh forgive me m'lady! this is all my fault! if only...
...if only i could go back in time and speak those fifteen magic words.
...grouped in five sets of three with a brief pause inbetween each set...
...things might've turned out very different!

MIGHT'VE?

THERE'S A LOT OF THINGS I WOULD CHANGE IF I COULD TRAVEL BACK IN TIME. BUT I CAN'T.
BECAUSE TIME TRAVEL IS IMPOSSIBLE.

NOT... NECESSARILY.

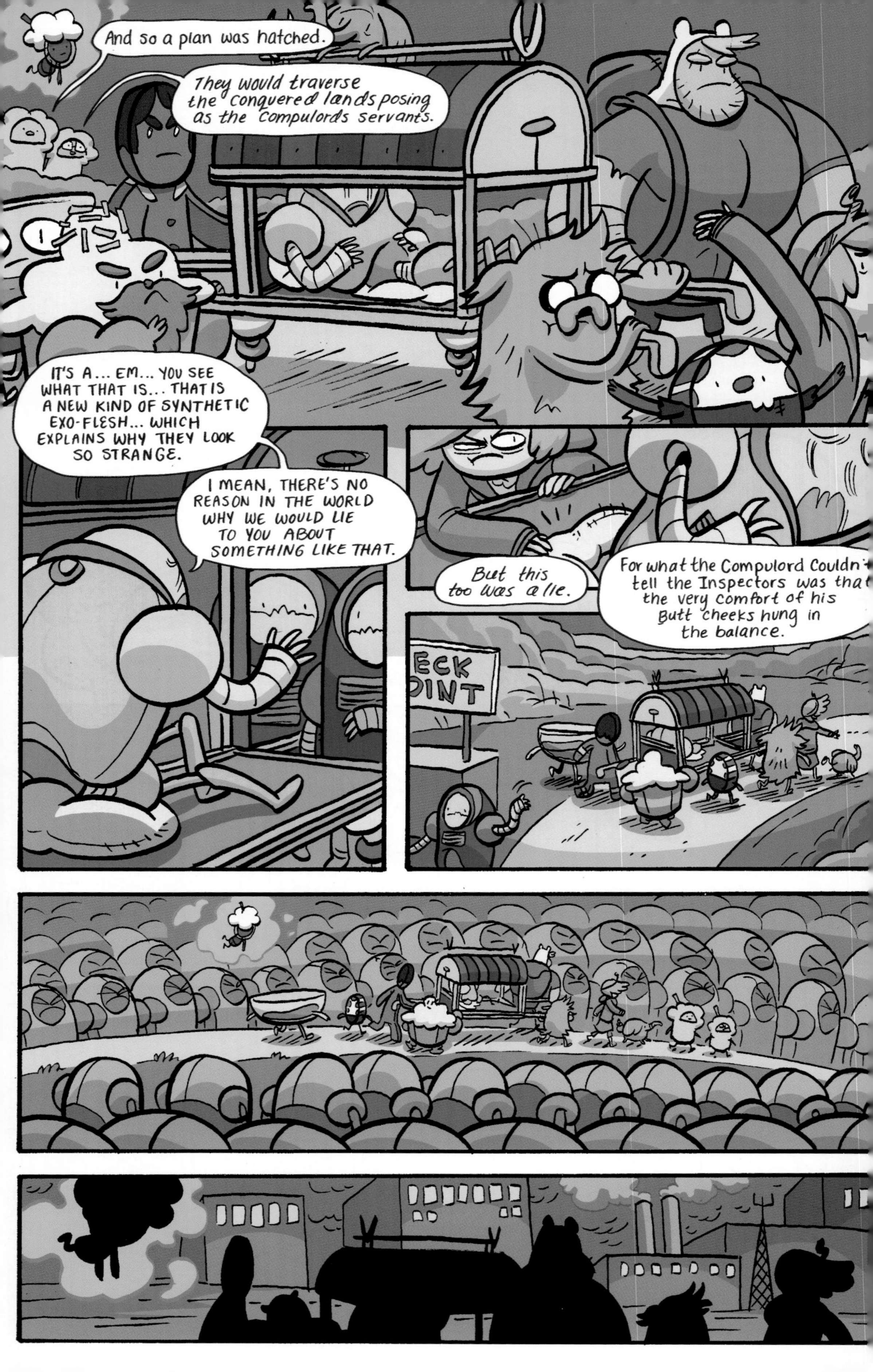

And so a plan was hatched.
They would traverse the conquered lands posing as the Compulord's servants.
!
IT'S A... EM... YOU SEE WHAT THAT IS... THAT IS A NEW KIND OF SYNTHETIC EXO-FLESH... WHICH EXPLAINS WHY THEY LOOK SO STRANGE.
I MEAN, THERE'S NO REASON IN THE WORLD WHY WE WOULD LIE TO YOU ABOUT SOMETHING LIKE THAT.
But this too was a lie.
For what the Compulord Couldn't tell the Inspectors was that the very comfort of his Butt cheeks hung in the balance.
ECK
OINT

THERE IT IS.
THE CITADEL OF TEMPORAL ATTUNEMENT.

NOT MUCH FURTHER NOW.

ALL WE HAVE TO DO IS CROSS THE TURNIP FIELDS, TALK OUR WAY PAST THE SECURITY GUARDS --

WAIT WAIT WAIT. DID YOU SAY...
... TURNIP FIELDS?

OF COURSE. WITHOUT BANANA GUARDS TO EAT THEM, THESE TURNIPS MUST'VE STARTED GROWING OUT OF CONTROL.
UHHNNGGG...
YUMMMMMY TURNIPS...
...oh yeah...
...Better than apples...
NOM NOM NOM...
So... good...
GUHHHH...
UHHHH...

THAT'S ALL OF 'EM. EXCEPT FOR THIS ONE THATS LOOKS LIKE LUMPY PRINCESS. ANYBODY WANT?
NUH-UH...
couldn't eat another bite...
I'm stuffed...
NO THANKS

HEY, LET ME ASK YOU GUYS SOMETHING.
IF YOU COULD GO BACK, KNOWING WHAT YOU KNOW NOW...
... WOULD YOU STILL BECOME BANANA GUARDS?

Oh no! Never! All I wanted was a nice hat, but I've learned there are far easier ways to get hats than joining The Banana Guard.

i had no business being a banana guard. it brought nothing but misery and death to this land.

NO WAY. I WAS A FOOL TO TRY TO BECOME SOMETHING I'M NOT. IF SHE CAN'T LOVE ME FOR WHO I AM, THEN IT WASN'T MEANT TO BE.
GLOB NO! I JUST WANTED TO STAY OUT OF JAIL.
Yes. In a heartbeat.
STOP
HONK
HONK
And so they all learned a valuable lesson.
They learned it's better to accept yourself for who you are than to try to become something you're not.
I want to become something I'm not.
DESPERATELY.
Uh... yes, except for Muto Bread.
He hadn't learned a thing.

OUR GREATEST CHALLENGE LIES AHEAD.
FOR TO GAIN ACCESS TO THE ATTUNEMENT SPHERE MANY OBSTACLES REMAIN IN OUR PATH.
SUPPOSING WE CAN TALK OUR WAY PAST THE GUARDS, WE WILL THEN PASS THROUGH A GAUNTLET OF LASER GRIDS, EACH GRID DEADLIER THAN THE LAST.
THEN COME THE MASHER BLADES... FIRE TUNNELS... FOLLOWED BY EIGHTY FLIGHTS OF RAZOR STAIRS... LEADING INTO A CLOUD OF MIND-CONTROL NANO BOTS THAT WILL STRIP YOUR FLESH TO THE BONE IF YOU FAIL EVEN A SINGLE TEST...
AND THAT'S JUST TO GET PAST THE FRONT GATE.
SUPPOSING YOU MAKE IT THAT FAR YOU WILL MOST LIKELY FIND YOURSELVES INSIDE ONE OF THE ATOMIC DISPLAY TUNNELS WHICH--
UM...
AND WE'RE ALL COOL WITH THIS?
IM COOL WITH IT
YEAH
ABSOLUTELY
totes
uh-huh
Nope not even a little.
YOU KNOW WHAT YOU HAVE TO DO

IN YOU GO!
BOOP!
must...focus...find the right universe...
thoughts... reality... coming into attunement... I see it... feel it...
ROOT BEER GUY
RRRR
RRRR
there it is! princess bubblegum's kitchen!
BLOOP

INSOMNIA IS OFTEN CAUSED BY INSUFFICIENT LEVELS OF MELATONIN IN THE BRAIN.
EATING FOODS RICH IN TRYPTOPHAN CAN GENERATE SEROTONIN, WHICH ENZYMES IN THE BRAIN CATALYZE INTO MELATONIN.
A TURNIP SANDWICH OUGHTA DO THE TRIC
GUM PHYSI
3
ASTROLO
IV
IIV
HOW?

TURNIPS... TURNIPS... TURNIPS...

AH. HERE WE GO!
I SHOULD BE ASLEEP IN NO TIME
The End

COVER GALLERY

ISSUE ONE COVER A
AIMEE FLECK

ISSUE TWO COVER A
AIMEE FLECK
BANANA GUARD
CADET
BANANA GUARD
CADET

ISSUE THREE COVER A
AIMEE FLECK
TUG ME

ISSUE FOUR COVER A
AIMEE FLECK

ISSUE FIVE COVER A
AIMEE FLECK

ISSUE SIX COVER A
AIMEE FLECK

ISSUE ONE COVER B
MICHELE PETRUCCI

ISSUE ONE COVE
NATALIE HA

ISSUE ONE SAN DIE
COMIC-CON EXCLUSI
COLEMAN ENGL

UE TWO COVER B
LSEY SUNDAY

ISSUE TWO COVER C
CAREY PIETSCH

SUE THREE COVER B
ENN LIV

ISSUE THREE COVER C
SYD BEE

ISSUE FOUR COVER B
CARREY PIETSCH

ISSUE FOUR COVER
PERRY MAP

ISSUE FIVE COVER
KATHLEEN LOLL

E FIVE COVER C
RY MAPLE

ISSUE SIX COVER B
CHRISTINA CHANG

UE SIX COVER C
LLIPE MARTINS

BOOM! STUDIOS EXCLUSIVE CONNECTING COVERS
KYLA VANDERKLUGT

TUG ME